W9-BHI-820

THE HOUSE ON THE CLIFF

"Maybe I can give you a tip where to find
your father," said Pretzel Pete

The Hardy Boys Mystery Stories®

THE HOUSE

ON

THE CLIFF

BY

FRANKLIN W. DIXON

SCHOLASTIC INC.
New York Toronto London Auckland Sydney

No part of this publication may be reproduced in whole or in part, or stored in a retrieval system, or transmitted in any form or by any means, electronic, mechanical, photocopying, recording or otherwise, without written permission of the publisher. For information regarding permission, write to Simon & Schuster, Inc., 1230 Avenue of the Americas, New York, NY 10020.

ISBN 0-590-46390-X

Copyright © 1987, 1959, 1955, 1927 by Simon & Schuster, Inc. All rights reserved. Published by Scholastic Inc., 730 Broadway, New York, NY 10003, by arrangement with Grosset & Dunlap, Inc., a division of The Putnam Berkeley Group, Inc., 200 Madison Avenue, New York, NY 10016. THE HARDY BOYS is a registered trademark of Simon & Schuster, Inc.

12 11 10 9 8 7 6 5 4 3 2 1   2 3 4 5 6 7/9

Printed in the U.S.A.   37

First Scholastic printing, October 1992

CONTENTS

THE HOUSE ON THE CLIFF

CHAPTER I

Spying by Telescope

"So you boys want to help me on another case?" Fenton Hardy, internationally known detective, smiled at his teen-age sons.

"Dad, you said you're working on a very mysterious case right now," Frank spoke up. "Isn't there some angle of it that Joe and I could tackle?"

Mr. Hardy looked out the window of his second-floor study as if searching for the answer somewhere in the town of Bayport, where the Hardys lived. Finally he turned back and gazed steadfastly at his sons.

"All right. How would you like to look for some smugglers?"

Joe Hardy's eyes opened wide. "You mean it, Dad?"

"Now just a minute." The detective held up his

hand. "I didn't say capture them; I just said look for them."

"Even that's a big assignment. Thanks for giving it to us!" Frank replied.

The lean, athletic detective walked to a corner of the study where a long, narrow carrying case stood. Tapping it, he said:

"You boys have learned how to manipulate this telescope pretty well. How would you like to take it out onto that high promontory above the ocean and train it seaward? The place I mean is two miles north of the end of the bay and eight miles from here."

"That would be great!" said seventeen-year-old, blond-haired Joe, his blue eyes flashing in anticipation.

Frank, who was a year older than his brother and less impetuous, asked in a serious tone of voice, "Dad, have you any ideas about the identity of any of the smugglers?"

"Yes, I do," Mr. Hardy answered his tall, dark-haired son. "I strongly suspect that a man named Felix Snattman is operating in this territory. I'll give you the whole story."

The detective went on to say that he had been engaged by an international pharmaceutical company to trace stolen shipments of valuable drugs. Reports of thefts had come from various parts of the United States. Local police had worked on the case, but so far had failed to apprehend any suspects.

"Headquarters of the firm is in India," the detective told the boys. "It was through them that I was finally called in. I'm sure that the thefts are the result of smuggling, very cleverly done. That's the reason I suspect Snattman. He's a noted criminal and has been mixed up in smuggling rackets before. He served a long term in prison, and after being released, dropped out of sight."

"And you think he's working around Bayport?" Joe asked. He whistled. "That doesn't make this town a very healthy place to live in!"

"But we're going to make it so!" Mr. Hardy declared, a ring of severity in his voice.

"Just where is this spot we're to use the telescope?" Frank asked eagerly.

"It's on the Pollitt place. You'll see the name at the entrance. An old man named Felix Pollitt lived there alone for many years. He was found dead in the house about a month ago, and the place has been vacant ever since."

"It sounds as if we could get a terrific range up and down the shore from there and many miles across the water," Frank remarked.

Mr. Hardy glanced at his wrist watch. "It's one-thirty now. You ought to be able to go out there, stay a fair amount of time, and still get home to supper."

"Oh, easily," Joe answered. "Our motorcycles can really burn up the road!"

His father smiled, but cautioned, "This telescope happens to be very valuable. The less jouncing it receives the better."

"I get the point," Joe conceded, then asked, "Dad, do you want us to keep the information about the smugglers to ourselves, or would it be all right to take a couple of the fellows along?"

"Of course I don't want the news broadcast," Mr. Hardy said, "but I know I can trust your special friends. Call them up."

"How about Chet and Biff?" Joe consulted Frank. As his brother nodded, he said, "You pack the telescope on your motorcycle. I'll phone."

Chet Morton was a stout, good-natured boy who loved to eat. Next to that, he enjoyed being with the Hardys and sharing their exciting adventures, although at times, when situations became dangerous, he wished he were somewhere else. Chet also loved to tinker with machinery and spent long hours on his jalopy which he called Queen. He was trying to "soup up" the motor, so that he could have a real "hot rod."

In contrast to Chet, Biff Hooper was tall and lanky. To the amusement—and wonder—of the other boys, he used his legs almost as a spider does, covering tremendous distances on level ground or vaulting fences.

A few minutes later Joe joined his brother in the garage and told him that both Chet and Biff would go along. Chet, he said, had apologized for not being able to offer the Queen for the trip but her engine was "all over the garage." "As usual," Frank said with a grin as the two boys climbed on their motorcycles and set out.

Presently the Hardys stopped at Biff Hooper's home. He ran out the door to meet them and climbed aboard behind Joe. Chet lived on a farm at the outskirts of Bayport, about a fifteen-minute run from the Hooper home. The stout boy had strolled down the lane to the road and was waiting for his friends. He hoisted himself onto Frank's motorcycle.

"I've never seen a powerful telescope in operation," he remarked. "How far away can you see with this thing?"

"It all depends on weather conditions," Frank replied. "On a clear day you can make out human figures at distances of twenty-four miles."

"Wow!" Chet exclaimed. "We ought to be able to find those smugglers easily."

"I wouldn't say so," Biff spoke up. "Smugglers have the same kind of boats as everybody else. How close do you have to be to identify a person?"

"Oh, about two and a half miles," Joe answered. The motorcycles chugged along the shore road, with Frank watching his speedometer carefully. "We ought to be coming to the Pollitt place soon," he said finally. "Keep your eyes open, fellows."

The boys rode on in silence, but suddenly they all exclaimed together, "There it is!"

At the entrance to a driveway thickly lined with trees and bushes was a stone pillar, into which the name "Pollitt" had been chiseled. Frank and Joe turned into the driveway. The only part of the house they could see was the top of the roof. Finally, beyond a lawn overgrown with weeds, they came upon the tall, rambling building. It stood like a beacon high above the water. Pounding surf could be heard far below.

"This place sure looks neglected," Biff remarked.

Dank, tall grass grew beneath the towering trees. Weeds and bushes threatened to engulf the whole building.

"Creepy, if you ask me," Chet spoke up. "I don't know why anybody would want to live here."

The house itself was in need of repair. Built of wood, it had several sagging shutters and the paint was flaking badly.

"Poor old Mr. Pollitt was probably too sick to take care of things," Frank commented, as he looked at several weed-choked flower beds.

To the Hardys' disappointment, the sky had

become overcast and they realized that visibility had been cut down considerably. Nevertheless, Frank unstrapped the carrying case and lugged it around to the front of the house.

He unfastened the locks and Joe helped his brother lift out the telescope and attached tripod, pulling up the eye-end section first.

Biff and Chet exclaimed in admiration.

"Boy, that's really neat!" Chet remarked.

He and Biff watched in fascination as Frank and Joe began to set up the telescope. First they unfastened the tape with which the tube and tripod legs were tied together. Joe turned the three legs down and pulled out the extensions to the desired height. Then Frank secured the tripod legs with a chain to keep them from spreading.

"What's next?" Biff asked.

"To get proper balance for the main telescope tube we slide it through this trunnion sleeve toward the eye end, like this." After doing so, Frank tightened the wing nuts on the tripod lightly.

Joe picked up the balance weight from the carrying case and screwed it into the right side of the telescope tube about one third the distance from the eyepiece.

"This'll keep the whole thing from being top heavy," he pointed out.

"And what's this little telescope alongside the big one for?" Chet queried.

"A finder," Frank explained. "Actually, it's a small guide telescope and helps the observer sight his big telescope on the object more easily."

"It's as clear as mud," Chet remarked with a

grin. He squinted through the ends of both the large and the small telescopes. "I can't see a thing," he complained.

Joe laughed. "And you won't until I insert one

of the eyepieces into the adapter of the big telescope and put another eyepiece into the finder."

In a few minutes the Hardys had the fascinating device working. By turning a small knob, Frank slowly swung the telescope from left to right, and each boy took a turn looking out across the water.

"Not a boat in sight!" said Chet, disappointed.

Frank had just taken his second turn squinting through the eyepiece when he called out excitedly, "I see something!"

He now began a running account of the scene he had just picked up. "It's not very clear . . . but I see a boat . . . must be at least six miles out."

"What kind of boat?" Joe put in.

"Looks like a cruiser . . . or a cutter. . . . It's not moving. . . . Want to take a look, Joe?"

Frank's brother changed places with him. "Say, fellows, a man's going over the side on a ladder . . . and, hey! there's a smaller boat down below. . . . He's climbing into it."

"Can you see a name or numbers on the big boat?" Frank asked excitedly.

"No. The boat's turned at a funny angle, so you can't see the lettering. You couldn't even if the weather was clearer."

"Which way is the man in the small boat heading?" Biff asked.

"He seems to be going toward Barmet Bay."

Joe gave up his position to Biff. "Suppose you keep your eye on him for a while, and also the big boat. Maybe it'll turn so you can catch the name or number on the box."

Chet had been silent for several moments. Now he said, "Do you suppose they're the smugglers?"

"Could be," Frank replied. "I think we'd better leave and report this to Dad from the first telephone we—"

He was interrupted by the sudden, terrifying scream of a man!

"Wh-where did that come from?" Chet asked with a frightened look.

"Sounded as if it came from inside," Frank answered.

The boys stared at the house on the cliff. A moment later they heard a loud cry for help. It was followed by another scream.

"Somebody's in there and is in trouble!" Joe exclaimed. "We'd better find out what's going on!"

Leaving the telescope, the four boys ran to the front door and tried the knob. The door was locked.

"Let's scatter and see if we can find another door," Frank suggested.

Frank and Joe took one side of the house, Biff and Chet the other. They met at the rear of the old home and together tried a door there. This, too, was locked.

"There's a broken window around the corner," Biff announced. "Shall we climb in?"

"I guess we'd better," Frank answered.

As the boys reached the window, which seemed to open into a library, they heard the scream again.

"Help! Hurry! Help!" came an agonized cry.

CHAPTER II

Thief at Work

JOE was first to slide through the broken window. "Wait a moment, fellows," he called out, "until I unlock this."

Quickly he turned the catch, raised the window, and the other three boys stepped inside the library. No one was there and they ran into the large center hall.

"Hello!" Frank shouted. "Where are you?"

There was no answer. "Maybe that person who was calling for help has passed out or is unconscious," Joe suggested. "Let's look around."

The boys dashed in various directions, and investigated the living room with its old-fashioned furnishings, the dining room with its heavily carved English oak set, the kitchen, and what had evidently been a maid's bedroom in days gone by. Now it was heaped high with empty boxes and crates. There was no one in any of the rooms and the Hardys and their two friends met again in the hall.

"The man must be upstairs," Frank decided.

He started up the front stairway and the others followed. There were several bedrooms. Suddenly Chet hung back. He wanted to go with his pals but the eeriness of the house made him pause. Biff and the Hardys sped from one to another of the many rooms. Finally they investigated the last of them.

"Nobody here! What do you make of it?" Biff asked, puzzled.

Chet, who had rejoined the group, said worriedly, "M-maybe the place is haunted!"

Joe's eyes were searching for an entrance to the third floor. Seeing none, he opened three doors in the hall, hoping to find a stairway. He saw none.

"There must be an attic in this house," he said. "I wonder how you get to it."

"Maybe there's an entrance from one of the bedrooms," Frank suggested. "Let's see."

The boys separated to investigate. Suddenly Frank called out, "I've found it."

The others ran to where he had discovered a door behind a man's shabby robe hanging inside a closet. This in turn revealed a stairway and the group hurriedly climbed it, Chet bringing up the rear.

The attic room was enormous. Old newspapers and magazines were strewn around among old-fashioned trunks and suitcases, but there was no human being in sight.

"I guess that cry for help didn't come from the house at all," Biff suggested. "What'll we do now? Look outdoors?"

"I guess we'll have to," Frank answered.

He started down the steep stairway. Reaching the foot, he turned the handle of the door which had swung shut. To his concern he was not able to open it.

"What's the matter?" asked Chet from the top of the stairway.

"Looks as if we're locked in," Frank told him.

"Locked in?" Chet wailed. "Oh, no!"

Frank tried pulling and pushing the door. It did not budge.

"That's funny," he said. "I didn't see any lock on the outside."

Suddenly the full import of the situation dawned on the four boys. Someone had deliberately locked them in! The cries for help had been a hoax to lure them into the house!

"You think somebody was playing a joke on us?" Biff asked.

"Pretty rotten kind of joke," Chet sputtered.

Frank and Joe were inclined to think that there was more to it than a joke. Someone had seen a chance to steal a valuable telescope and two late-model motorcycles!

"We've got to get out of here!" Joe said. "Frank, put your shoulder to the door and I'll help."

Fortunately, the door was not particularly sturdy and gave way easily. Frank glanced back a moment as he rushed through and saw two large hooks which he had not noticed before. They had evidently been slipped into the eyes and had been ripped from the framework by the crash on the door.

The other boys followed, running pell-mell through the hallway and clattering down the stairway. They dashed out the front door, leaving it open behind them. To their relief, the telescope still stood at the edge of the cliff, pointing seaward.

"Thank goodness!" said Joe. "I'd hate to have had to tell Dad the telescope was gone!"

Frank rushed over to take a quick look through the instrument. It had occurred to him that maybe some confederate of the smugglers had seen them spying. He might even have tricked them into the house during the very time that a smuggling operation would be within range of the telescope!

When Frank reached the edge of the cliff and tried to look through the instrument, he gasped in dismay. The eyepieces from both the finder and the telescope tube had been removed!

As he turned to tell the other boys of his discovery, he found that they were not behind him. But a moment later Joe came running around the corner of the house calling out:

"The motorcycles are safe! Nobody stole them!"

"Thank goodness for that," said Frank.

Chet and Biff joined them and all flopped down on the grass to discuss the mysterious happenings and work out a plan of action.

"If that thief is hiding inside the house, I'm going to find him," Joe declared finally.

"I'm with you," said Frank, jumping up. "How about you, Biff, guarding the motorcycles and Chet taking charge of the telescope? That way, both the front and back doors will be covered, too, in case that thief comes out."

"Okay," the Hardys' friends agreed.

As Frank and Joe entered the front hall, Joe remarked, "There's a back stairway. If we don't find the person on the first floor, I'll take that to the second. You take the front."

Frank nodded and the search began. Not only the first, but the second and attic floors were thoroughly investigated without results.

"There's only one place left," said Frank. "The cellar."

This area also proved to have no one hiding

in it. "I guess our thief got away," Frank stated.

"And probably on foot," Joe added. "I didn't hear any car, did you?"

"No. Maybe he went down the cliff and made a getaway in a boat," Frank suggested.

In complete disgust the Hardys reported their failure to Biff and Chet. Then they packed up the telescope and strapped it onto Frank's motorcycle.

"We may as well go home," Joe said dolefully. "We'll have a pretty slim report for Dad."

"Slim?" said Biff. "I haven't had so much excitement in six months."

The boys climbed aboard the motorcycles. As the Hardys were about to start the motors, all four of them froze in the seats. From somewhere below the cliff came a demoniacal laugh. Involuntarily the boys shuddered.

"L-let's get out of here!" Chet urged.

Frank and Joe had hopped off the motorcycles, and were racing in the direction from which the eerie laughter was coming.

"It may be another trap!" Chet yelled after them. "Come back!"

But the Hardys went on. Just before they reached the edge of the cliff they were thunderstruck to hear the laughter coming from a completely different area. It was actually in back of them!

"What gives?" Joe asked.

"Search me," his brother answered. "The ghost must have a confederate."

The brothers peered over the edge of the cliff but could see only jagged rocks that led to the booming surf below. Frank and Joe returned to their chums, disappointed that they had learned nothing and had no explanation for the second laugh.

"I'm glad it stopped, anyhow," said Chet. "It gave me goose pimples and made chills run up and down my spine."

Biff looked at his wrist watch. "I really have to be getting home, fellows. Sorry to break up this man hunt. Maybe you can take me to a bus and come back."

The Hardys would not hear of this and said they would leave at once.

They had gone scarcely a mile when the motor on Frank's cycle sputtered and backfired, then died. "A swell time for a breakdown," he said disgustedly as he honked for Joe to stop.

Joe turned around and drove back. "What's the matter?"

"Don't know." Frank dismounted. "It's not the gas. I have plenty of that."

"Tough luck!" Joe said sympathetically. "Well, let's take a look at the motor. Better get out your tools."

As Frank opened the toolbox of his motorcycle, an expression of bewilderment came over his face.

"My tools!" he exclaimed. "They're gone!"

The others gathered around. The toolbox was indeed empty!

"Are you sure you had them when you left Bayport?" Chet asked.

"Of course I did. I never go anywhere without them."

Biff shook his head. "I suppose the guy who took the eyepieces stole your tools too."

Joe dashed to the toolbox on his own motorcycle and gave a cry of dismay.

"Mine are gone, too!"

CHAPTER III

Landslide!

"THAT'S a shame, fellows," Chet Morton said. "This is sure your day for bad luck. First the eye-pieces from your telescope are taken and now the tools from your motorcycles."

"And all by the same person, I'm sure," Frank remarked grimly.

"Some slick operator, whoever he is," Joe added gloomily.

Chet put his hands into his trouser pockets and with a grin pulled out a pair of pliers, a screw driver, and a wrench.

"I was working on the Queen this morning," he explained. "Good thing I happened to put these in my pocket."

"I'll say," Frank declared gratefully, taking the tools which Chet handed over.

He unfastened the housing of the motor and

began checking every inch of the machinery. Finally he looked up and announced, "I guess I've found the trouble—a loose connection."

Frank adjusted the wires and a moment later the vehicle's motor was roaring normally. The housing was put back on, Chet's tools were returned with thanks, and the four boys set off once more.

"Let's hope nothing more happens before we get home," Biff said with a wry laugh.

"I'll second that," Joe said emphatically.

For five minutes the cyclists rode along in silence, their thoughts partly on the passing scenery, but mostly on the mystery in which they had become involved.

Joe's mind was racing with his throbbing motorcycle. In a few minutes he had far outdistanced his brother. Frank did not dare go any faster because of the telescope strapped onto his handle bars.

Presently Joe reached a spot in the road where it had been cut out of the hillside on the right. There was a sharp curve here. The motorcycle took it neatly, but he and Biff had scarcely reached the straightaway beyond when they heard a thunderous sound back of them.

"What's that?" Joe cried out.

Biff turned to look over his shoulder. "A landslide!" he shouted.

Rocks and dirt, loosened by recent heavy rainstorms, were tumbling down the steep hillside at terrific speed.

"Frank!" Joe cried out in horror. He jammed on his brake and disengaged the engine. As he ran back to warn his brother, Joe saw that he was too late. Biff had rushed up and both could only stare helplessly, their hearts sinking.

Frank and Chet came around the corner at good speed and ran full tilt into the landslide. Its rumbling sound had been drowned out by the pounding surf and their own roaring motor.

The two boys, the motorcycle, and the telescope were bowled over by the falling rocks and earth. As the rain of debris finally stopped, Joe and Biff reached their sides.

"Frank! Chet!" they cried out in unison. "Are you hurt?"

Frank, then Chet, sat up slowly. Aside from looking a bit dazed, they seemed to be all right. "Rock just missed my head," Frank said finally.

"I got a mean wallop on my shoulder," Chet panted gingerly, rubbing the sore spot.

"You fellows were lucky," Biff spoke up, and Joe nodded his intense relief.

"How about the telescope?" Frank asked quickly. "Take a look at it, will you, Joe?"

The battered carrying case, pushed out of the straps which had held it in place on the motorcycle, lay in the road, covered with stone and dirt. Joe opened the heavily lined box and carefully examined the telescope.

"It looks all right to me," he said in a relieved voice. "Of course we won't know for sure until we try other eyepieces in it. But at least nothing looks broken."

By this time Frank and Chet were standing up and Biff remarked, "While you two are getting your breath, Joe and I can take the biggest rocks out of the way. Some motorist may come speeding along here and break his neck or wreck his car unless this place gets cleaned up."

"Oh, I'm okay," Chet insisted. "The rock that hit me felt just like Bender, that big end on the Milton High team. He's hit me many a time the same way."

Frank, too, declared that he felt no ill effects. Together, the boys flung rock after rock into the field between the road and the water and, in pairs, carried the heavier rocks out of the way.

"Guess we're all set now," Frank spoke up. "Biff, I'm afraid you're going to be late getting home." He chuckled. "Who is she?"

Biff reddened a little. "How'd you guess? I have a date tonight with Sally Sanderson. But she's a good sport. She won't mind waiting a little longer."

Again the four boys straddled the motorcycles

and started off. A few minutes later a noise out in the ocean attracted Frank's attention and he peered across the rolling sweep of waters. A powerful speedboat came into view around the base of a small cliff about a quarter mile out. It was followed at a short distance by a similar, but larger craft. Both boats were traveling at high speed.

"Looks like a race!" Joe called out. "Let's watch it!"

The Hardys ran their motorcycles behind a clump of trees and stopped, then walked down to the shore line.

The boats did not appear to be having a friendly speed contest, however. The first boat was zigzagging in a peculiar manner, and the pursuing craft was rapidly overtaking it.

"See! That second boat is trying to stop the other one!" Frank exclaimed.

"It sure is. Wonder what's up," said Joe tensely. "I wish that telescope was working. Can any of you fellows make out the names on the boats?"

"No," the others chorused.

The two men standing in the bow of the pursuing craft were waving their arms frantically. The first boat turned as if about to head toward the shore. Then, apparently, the helmsman changed his mind, for at once the nose of his boat was pointed out into the ocean again.

But the moment of hesitation had given the

pursuers the chance they needed. Swiftly the gap between the racing craft grew smaller and smaller until the boats were running side by side. They were so close together that a collision seemed imminent.

"They'll all be killed if they aren't careful!" Frank muttered as he watched intently.

The lone man in the foremost craft was bent over the wheel. In the boat behind, one of the two men suddenly raised his right arm high. A moment later he hurled an object through the air. It landed in back of the engine housing in the center of the craft. At the same time the larger boat sped off seaward.

"What was that?" Chet asked. "I—"

Suddenly a sheet of flame leaped high into the air from the smaller boat. There was a stunning explosion and a dense cloud of smoke rose in the air. Bits of wreckage were thrown high and in the midst of it the boys saw the occupant hurled into the water.

Swiftly the whole boat caught fire. The flames raced from bow to stern.

"That man!" shouted Frank. "He's alive!"

The boys could see him struggling in the surf, trying to swim ashore.

"He'll never make it!" Joe gasped. "He's all in."

"We've got to save him!" Frank cried out.

CHAPTER IV

The Rescue

THE Hardy boys knew that they had no time to lose. It was evident that the man in the water had been injured by the explosion and could not swim much longer.

"We'll never reach him!" Chet said, as the four boys dashed across the rocks and grass to the shore.

Suddenly Frank cried out, "I see a rowboat up on the beach." His sharp eyes had detected a large rowboat almost completely hidden in a small cove at the bottom of the cliff. "We'd make better time in that!"

A huge rock jutting out of the water cut the cove off from the open part of the beach.

"We'd have to go up to that ridge and then down," Joe objected. "I'll swim out."

"I will too," said Biff.

The two plunged into the water and struck out for the stricken man.

Meanwhile, Frank and Chet sped up the slope, cut across a strip of grass, and began running down the embankment toward the rowboat.

"That man's still afloat," Frank shouted as he looked out over the water.

Joe and Biff were making good time but were a long way from the man, who seemed now to be drifting with the outgoing tide. The explosion victim, fortunately, had managed to seize a piece of wreckage and was hanging onto it.

Slipping and scrambling, Frank and Chet made their way down the slope. Rocks rolled and tumbled ahead of them. But finally they reached the bottom safely and examined the boat. It was battered and old, but evidently still seaworthy. There were two sets of oars.

"Grab hold!" Frank directed Chet.

The boys pulled the boat across the pebbles and into the water. Swiftly they fixed the oars in the locks and took their places. Pulling hard, Frank and Chet rowed toward the distressed swimmer. Presently they overtook Joe and Biff, who clambered aboard. The man had seen the boys and called feebly to them to hurry.

"Faster!" Joe urged. "He looks as if he'll go under any second!"

The motorboat in the background was still

blazing fiercely, flames shooting high in the air. The craft was plainly doomed.

The boys pulled harder and the rowboat leaped across the water. When it was only a few yards away from the man, he suddenly let go his hold on the bit of wreckage and slipped beneath the waves.

"He's drowning!" Chet shouted, as he bent to his oar again.

Joe made a tremendously long, outward dive and disappeared into the water where the man had gone down. Frank and Chet rowed the boat to the spot and leaned over the side to peer down.

Just then, Joe and the stranger broke the surface of the water, with the boy holding an arm under the man's shoulders. His head sagged.

"He's unconscious!" Biff whispered hoarsely, as he helped pull the victim into the boat. The man sprawled helplessly on the bottom, more dead than alive.

"We'd better revive him and get him to the hospital," said Frank.

He applied artificial respiration, forcing a little water from the man's lungs, but the stranger did not regain consciousness.

"I think he collapsed from exhaustion," Joe spoke up.

Frank and Chet took off their jackets and wrapped them around the wet figure.

"How about taking him to that farmhouse over there—along the road?" Chet suggested.

The others agreed. As Frank and Chet rowed toward the farm, the boys discussed the mystery. Who was the victim of the explosion and why had the men in the other motorboat tried to kill him?

The man they had rescued lay face downward in the bottom of the boat. He was a slim, dark-haired man with sharp, clean-cut features, and his clothes were cheap and worn. Biff looked in his pockets for identification but found none.

"Wonder if he's a local man," Joe said. "Never saw him around town."

The other boys declared they never had either.

By this time the boat was close to shore. Joe and Biff leaped out and dragged it part way up on the beach. Then the four boys carried the unconscious man up the rocky shore toward the farmhouse.

At their approach a plump woman came hurrying out of the house. From the orchard nearby a burly man in overalls came forward.

"My goodness! What has happened?" the woman asked, running toward them.

"We just pulled this man out of the water," Frank explained. "We saw your house—"

"Bring him in," boomed the farmer. "Bring him right in."

The woman ran ahead and held the door

open. The boys carried the stranger into the
house and laid him on a bed in the comfortably
furnished first-floor bedroom. The farmer's wife
hastened to the kitchen to prepare a hot drink.

"Rub his ankles and wrists, and get those wet
clothes off him," the farmer told the boys. "That
will step up his circulation. I'll get him some pa-
jamas."

"How about calling a doctor?" Frank asked.

"No need. He'll be okay," the farmer declared.

The victim was soon under the covers. Frank
and Joe continued to massage his wrists and ankles.

At last the stranger stirred feebly. His eyelids
fluttered. His lips moved, but no words came.
Then his eyes opened and the man stared at those
around him, as though in a daze.

"Where am I?" he muttered faintly.

"You're safe," Frank assured him. "You're with
friends."

"You saved me?"

"Yes."

"Pretty near—cashed in—didn't I?"

"You nearly drowned, but you're all right now.
When you feel like talking, you can tell us the
whole story," said Frank. "But, in the meantime,
we'll call the police or the Coast Guard and report
those men who tried to murder you."

The man in the bed blinked and looked out the

window. Finally he said, "No, no. Don't do that."

The boys were shocked. "Why not?" Joe burst out.

The man was thoughtfully silent for a moment, then said, "Thanks, but I'd rather let matters stand as they are. I'll take care of it as soon as I get my strength back." The rescued man turned to the farmer. "Okay with you if I stay here overnight? I'll pay you, of course."

The farmer put out his hand. "The name's Kane and you're welcome to stay until you feel strong. Nobody can say I ever turned a sick man away. And what's your name?"

The patient hesitated a moment. "Jones. Bill Jones," he said at last.

It was so evidently a false name that the Hardys glanced knowingly at each other. Mr. Kane did not seem to realize that his guest was apparently trying to hide his identity.

Mrs. Kane appeared with hot broth and toast. She suggested that her husband and the boys let the patient rest for a while. When she joined them in the living room she invited the boys to have a snack. Chet readily accepted for all of them.

The snack consisted of sandwiches of home-cured ham with cheese, glasses of fresh milk, and rich lemon pie, frothy with meringue. Chet beamed. "Mrs. Kane, you ought to open a restaurant. I'd be a steady customer. You're the best pie maker I've ever met."

Frank, Joe, and Biff chuckled. How often they had heard their stout, food-loving chum make similar remarks! But in this case they had to agree with him and told Mrs. Kane so.

She smiled. "It's the least I can do for you boys who just saved someone's life."

Her young guests said nothing of their early afternoon's adventure inside the Pollitt house, but Frank casually asked the Kanes if they had known the deceased owner and if anyone were living there now.

"Sure I knew Felix Pollitt," the farmer replied. "Closemouthed old codger, but I did hear him once say somethin' about havin' a no-good nephew. Pollitt said he was his only livin' relative and he supposed he'd have to leave the property to him."

"But who'd want the place?" Mrs. Kane spoke up. "It's falling apart and would cost a mint of money to fix up."

Joe grinned. "Sounds like a haunted house," he remarked pointedly.

"Funny you should say that." Mrs. Kane looked at Joe. "There was a family stopped here the other day. Wanted to buy some eggs. One of the little girls said they'd had a terrible scare. They'd stopped at the old Pollitt place to have a picnic, and were scared out of their wits by moans and groans and queer laughs from the house."

Mr. Kane's face broke into a grin. "The kid's imagination sure was runnin' away with itself."

"I'm not so sure of that," his wife disagreed. "I think some boys were in there playing pranks."

After Frank and Joe and their friends had left the farmhouse, they discussed the strange noises at the Pollitt place from this new angle.

Biff frowned. "If those ghosts are from Bayport High, they'll sure have the laugh on us," he remarked.

"They sure will," Chet agreed. "I'd hate to face them on Monday."

Frank and Joe were not convinced. After they had dropped their chums at the Morton and Hooper homes, they discussed the day's strange and varied adventures all the way to the Hardy house.

"I'm sure that ghost business was meant to be something more than a prank," Frank stated.

"Right," his brother agreed. "I just had an idea, Frank. Maybe nobody was in the house, but he could have rigged up a tape recorder to make those sounds and a remote control to start it. What say we go back sometime and take a look?"

"I'm with you."

By this time the boys had turned into the long driveway of the Hardy home, a spacious, three-story clapboard house on the corner of High and Elm streets. The large two-story garage at the rear of an attractive garden had once been a barn.

Frank and Joe parked their motorcycles, unstrapped the telescope, and carried it to the back porch. As they entered the kitchen, they found their mother, a pretty, sweet-faced woman, with sparkling blue eyes, preparing supper.

"Hello, boys," she greeted them. "Did you have a good day? See any smugglers?"

They kissed her and Frank said, "We have a lot to tell you and Dad."

"He's in the study upstairs. I'll go up with you right away and we can talk while the chicken's roasting and the potatoes baking."

The three hurried up to the room where Mr. Hardy was busy looking in a large metal file in which he kept important records. The detective stopped his work and listened with rapt attention as Frank and Joe gave a detailed account of their adventures.

"We sure fell for that cry for help," Joe explained. "I'm sorry about the stolen eyepieces from the telescope."

"And I hope it wasn't damaged when I had my spill," Frank added. He smiled wanly. "You'll probably want to dismiss us from your detective force."

"Nothing of the kind," his father said. "But

now, let's discuss what you saw through the telescope. You said you spotted a man who climbed down the ladder of a boat and went off in a smaller one. Could he have been this same fellow who calls himself Jones?"

"We couldn't identify him," Joe replied, "but he might be."

Frank snapped his fingers. "Yes, and he could be one of the smugglers."

"But who threw that hand grenade at him?" Joe asked. "Not one of his own gang, surely. And those guys in the other speedboat—they couldn't have been Coast Guard men, even in disguise. They wouldn't use grenades."

"Joe's right on the second point," Mr. Hardy agreed. "But Jones may still be a smuggler."

"You mean he might have done something to make his boss mad and the boss sent out a couple of men to get him?" Joe asked.

The detective nodded. "If this theory is right, and we can persuade Jones to talk before he either rejoins the gang or starts trying to take revenge, then we might get him to turn state's evidence."

The boys were excited. Both jumped from their chairs and Joe cried out eagerly, "Let's go talk to him right away! By morning he'll be gone!"

CHAPTER V

Pretzel Pete

"Just a minute!" Mrs. Hardy said to her sons. "How about supper?"

"We can eat when we come back from our interview with Jones," Joe answered. "Mother, he may decide to leave the farmhouse any time."

Despairingly Mrs. Hardy returned to her husband. "What do you think, Fenton?"

The detective gave his wife an understanding smile, then turned to Frank and Joe. "Didn't you say Jones was in pretty bad shape?"

"Yes, Dad," Frank replied.

"Then I doubt very much that he'll try to leave the Kanes' home before the time he set—tomorrow morning. I'm sure that it'll be safe for us to eat Mother's good supper and still see our man in time."

Joe subsided, and to make his mother feel better, said with a smile, "Guess I let this mystery go to my brain for a minute. As a matter of fact, I have an empty space inside of me big enough to eat two suppers!"

Mrs. Hardy tweaked an ear of her energetic son, just as she had frequently done ever since he was a small boy. He smiled at her affectionately, then asked what he could do to help with supper.

"Well, suppose you fill the water glasses and get milk for you and Frank," Mrs. Hardy said, as she and Joe went downstairs together.

At the table, as often happened at meals in the Hardy home, the conversation revolved around the mystery. Frank asked his father if he had made any progress on his part in the case concerning the smugglers.

"Very little," the detective replied. "Snattman is a slippery individual. He covers his tracks well. I did find this out, though. The law firm which is handling old Mr. Pollitt's affairs has had no luck in locating the nephew to whom the property was left."

"Mr. Kane said he'd heard Mr. Pollitt call his nephew a no-good," Frank put in.

"That's just the point," Mr. Hardy said. "The lawyers learned from the police that he's a hoodlum and is wanted for burglary."

Frank whistled. "That puts the nephew in a

bad spot, doesn't it? If he shows up to claim the property, he'll be nabbed as a criminal."

"Exactly," Mr. Hardy answered.

"What will become of the property?" Joe queried.

His father said he thought the executors might let the house remain vacant or they might possibly rent it. "They could do this on a month-to-month basis. This would give added income to the estate."

"Which wouldn't do the nephew much good if he were in jail," Mrs. Hardy put in.

"That would depend on how long his sentence was," her husband said. "He may not be a dangerous criminal. He may just have fallen into bad company and unwittingly become an accessory in some holdup or burglary."

"In that case," Frank remarked, "he may realize that he wouldn't have to stay in prison long. He may appear to claim the property, take his punishment, and then lead a normal, law-abiding life out at his uncle's place."

"Well, I sincerely hope so," Mr. Hardy replied. "The trouble is, so often when a young man joins a group of hoodlums or racketeers, he's blackmailed for the rest of his life, even though he tries to go straight." The detective smiled. "The best way to avoid such a situation is never to get into it!"

At this moment the phone rang and Frank went to answer it. "It's for you, Dad!" he called, coming back to the table.'

Mr. Hardy spent nearly fifteen minutes in conversation with the caller. In the meantime, the boys and Mrs. Hardy finished their supper. Then, while Mr. Hardy ate his dessert, he told his family a little about the information he had just received on the phone.

"More drugs have disappeared," he said tersely. "I'm positive now that Snattman is behind all this."

"Were the drugs stolen around here?" Frank asked.

"We don't know," his father answered. "A pharmaceutical house in the Midwest was expecting a shipment of rare drugs from India. When the package arrived, only half the order was there. It was evident that someone had cleverly opened the package, removed part of the shipment, and replaced the wrapping so neatly that neither the customs officials nor the post office was aware that the package had been tampered with."

"How were the drugs sent to this country?" Joe queried.

"They came by ship."

"To which port?"

"New York. But the ship did stop at Bayport."

"How long ago was this?"

"Nearly two months ago. It seems that the pharmaceutical house wasn't ready to use the drugs until now, so hadn't opened the package."

"Then," said Joe, "the drugs could have been removed right on the premises, and have had nothing to do with smugglers."

"You're right," Mr. Hardy agreed. "Each time drugs are reported missing, there's a new angle to the case. Although I'm convinced Snattman is back of it, how to prove this is really a stickler."

Mr. Hardy went on to say that the tip he had received about Snattman being in the Bayport area had been a very reliable one. He smiled. "I'll tell you all a little secret. I have a very good friend down on the waterfront. He picks up many kinds of information for me. His name is Pretzel Pete."

"Pretzel Pete!" Frank and Joe cried out. "What a name!"

"That's his nickname along the waterfront," Mr. Hardy told them. He laughed. "During the past few years I've munched on so many of the pretzels he sells, I think I'm his best customer."

By this time the boys' father had finished his dessert, and he suggested they leave at once for the Kane farmhouse. He brought his black sedan from the garage and the boys hopped in. It did not take long to cover the six miles to the place where Jones was spending the night.

"Why, the house is dark," Frank remarked, puzzled.

"Maybe everyone's asleep," Joe suggested.

"*This* early?" Frank protested.

Mr. Hardy continued on down the lane. There was no sign of anyone around the place. Frank remarked that perhaps the farmer and his wife had gone out for the evening. "But I'm surprised that they would leave Jones alone in his condition," he added.

"I'm quite sure they wouldn't," his father averred. "If they're asleep, I'm afraid we'll have to wake them."

He pulled up in front of the kitchen entrance. Frank was out of the car in an instant, the others followed. He rapped on the door. There was no answer.

"Let's try the front door," Joe suggested. "Maybe that has a knocker on it."

The boys walked around to the ocean side of the house. Although they banged loudly with the brass door knocker, there was still no response.

"The Kanes must have gone out," said Joe.

"But what about Jones? Surely he's here."

"And too weak to come to the door," Frank surmised. "But he *could* call out. I can't understand it."

The brothers returned to the back door and reported to their father. Then, as Joe rapped several more times without response, a sinking feeling came over the brothers.

"I guess Jones recovered fast and has gone," Joe said dejectedly. "We've goofed."

"Try the knob. The door may not be locked," Mr. Hardy ordered. From his tone the boys knew that he shared their fears.

Frank turned the knob and the door swung open. Mr. Hardy felt around for a light switch on the wall.

"We'll go in," he murmured. "If Jones is here we'll talk to him."

By this time the detective had found the switch. As the kitchen became flooded with light, the boys gasped, thunderstruck. On their previous visit they had been impressed by the neatness of the room. Now the place looked as though an earthquake had shaken it.

Pots and pans were scattered about the floor. The table was overturned. A chair lay upside down in a corner. Shattered bits of cups and saucers were strewn on the floor.

"What happened?" Frank exclaimed in bewilderment.

"There's been a fight—or a struggle of some kind," said Mr. Hardy. "Let's see what the rest of the house looks like."

The boys opened the door to the adjoining living room. Frank snapped on the wall switch.

The farmer and his wife were bound and gagged

There a horrifying sight met the Hardys' eyes.

The farmer and his wife, bound and gagged, were tied to chairs in the middle of the room!

Swiftly Frank, Joe, and their father rushed over to Mr. and Mrs. Kane. They had been tied with strong ropes and so well gagged that the couple had been unable to utter a sound. In a minute the Hardys had loosened the bonds and removed the gags.

"Thank goodness!" Mrs. Kane exclaimed with a sigh of relief, stretching her arms.

Her husband, spluttering with rage, rose from his chair and hurled the ropes to one side. "Those scoundrels!" he cried out.

Frank hastily introduced his father, then asked, "What happened?"

For several moments Mr. and Mrs. Kane were too upset to tell their story. But finally the farmer staggered over to the window and pointed down the shore road.

"They went that way!" he roared. "Follow them!"

"Who?"

"Those thugs who tied us up! They took Jones!"

CHAPTER VI

The Strange Message

"How long ago did those kidnapers leave?" Frank asked the Kanes quickly.

"About ten minutes," replied the farmer. "Maybe you can catch them if you hurry!"

"Come on, Dad!" Frank cried. "Let's go after them!"

Mr. Hardy needed no further urging. He and his sons ran out of the house and jumped into the car.

"That's rough stuff," Joe said to his father as they turned onto the shore road, "barging into a house, tying up the owners, and kidnaping a guy!"

"Yes," Mr. Hardy agreed. "It looks as though your friend Jones *is* mixed up in some kind of racket. Those men must have been pretty desperate to risk breaking into an occupied house."

The boys' father was able to follow the tracks of the car from the tread marks in the dusty road. But soon there were signs that another car had turned onto the shore road from a side lane and the trail became confused.

The Hardys passed the lane that led into the Pollitt place and continued on until they came to a hilltop. Here they could get a clear view of the road winding along the coast for several miles. There was no sign of a car.

"We've lost them, I guess," said Frank in disappointment, as Mr. Hardy brought the sedan to a stop.

"They had too much of a head start," Joe remarked. "If only we'd gotten to the farm sooner. Well, we may as well go back."

Mr. Hardy agreed, turned the car around, and once more the Hardys headed for the farm. On the way they discussed the mysterious kidnaping, and speculated on the identity of those responsible.

"I'll bet those men in the other motorboat saw us rescue Jones, or else they heard somehow that he'd been taken to the farmhouse," Joe surmised.

"If they *are* the kidnapers, I wonder what will happen to Jones now," Frank said gravely. "They tried to kill him once."

"Maybe they'll just hold him prisoner," Mr. Hardy stated thoughtfully. "They were probably afraid he'd tell all he knew, and couldn't afford to leave him at the farmhouse."

When they got back to the Kanes', they found the farmer and his wife somewhat recovered from their harrowing experience. Mrs. Kane was busy straightening up the kitchen.

"We couldn't catch them," Frank reported sadly.

"Well, those hoodlums had a high-powered car and they weren't wastin' any time. I could see 'em from the window as they went down the lane," the farmer remarked, frowning angrily at the recollection.

"Please tell us exactly what happened, Mr. Kane," Joe urged.

"Well, Mabel and I were here in the kitchen," the man began. "Mabel was washin' the supper dishes when this fellow came to the door. He was a tall chap with a long, thin face."

"He asked us if we were looking after the man that was almost drowned earlier," the farmer's wife took up the tale. "When we said we were, the fellow told us that Mr. Jones was his brother and he had come to take him away."

"I got suspicious," Mr. Kane broke in. "He didn't look nothin' like Jones. I asked him where he lived."

"At that," Mrs. Kane said, "he walked in the house with another fellow right at his heels.

They grabbed my husband. Henry put up an awful good fight but he was outnumbered. When I tried to help, a third man appeared from no-where and held me back."

"They dragged us into the livin' room, tied us to those chairs, and put the gags in our mouths," the farmer continued. "Then we heard 'em goin' into Jones's room. Pretty soon they carried him out to a car where a fourth fellow was sittin' at the wheel."

"Did Jones put up a fight when they took him away?" Frank asked.

"He tried to. He hollered for help, but of course I couldn't do anythin' and he was too weak to struggle much."

"This whole affair is very peculiar," Mr. Hardy observed. "Perhaps Jones is mixed up in the smuggling going on around here. But who were those four men, I wonder?"

Mrs. Kane shook her head. "All I know is, we're sure glad you and your sons came out to-night. There's no telling how long we'd have been tied up before somebody found us!"

"We're glad, too, that we got here," Frank replied.

"You folks say your name's Hardy?" said the farmer. "Any relation to Fenton Hardy?"

"Right here." The detective smiled.

"Pleasure to know you!" exclaimed Kane

heartily, putting out his hand. "If anyone can get to the bottom of this business, you can."

"I'll certainly try," the boys' father promised.

The Hardys bade the farmer and his wife good-by. They promised to call again at the Kane farm as soon as they had any further information, and Mr. Kane, in turn, said he would notify them if he found any trace of Jones or his kidnapers.

When they returned home the boys followed their father into his study.

"What do you make of all this, Dad?" Joe asked.

Mr. Hardy sat down at his desk. He closed his eyes and leaned back in his chair a few moments without speaking.

"I have only one theory," he said at last. "The kidnapers probably are Snattman's friends. That means you boys may have uncovered the fact that there is a whole gang of smugglers around here."

The brothers were pleased with their progress. "What do we do next, Dad?" Joe asked eagerly.

"I want to evaluate this case from every angle," their father replied. "I'll think about it and talk to you later." With this the boys had to be content for the rest of the week end.

When the brothers came downstairs Monday morning, Mrs. Hardy was putting their breakfast on the table.

In answer to the boys' inquiries, she replied, "Your father went out early this morning in his car. He didn't say when he would return. But your dad didn't take a bag with him, so he'll probably be back today." Mrs. Hardy was accustomed to her husband's comings and goings at odd hours in connection with his profession and she had learned not to ask questions.

Frank and Joe were disappointed. They had looked forward to resuming a discussion of the case with their father.

"I guess we're left on our own again to try finding out something about those smugglers," Frank remarked, and Joe agreed.

Later, when they reached Bayport High School, the brothers saw Iola Morton standing on the front steps. With pretty, dark-haired Iola was her best friend Callie Shaw. Callie, a blond, vivacious, brown-eyed girl, was Frank's favorite among all the girls in his class.

"How are the ghost hunters this morning?" she asked with a mischievous smile. "Iola told me about your adventures on Saturday."

"Chet was really scared," Iola chimed in. "I think somebody played a good joke on all of you."

"Well, whoever it was had better return the telescope eyepieces and our motorcycle tools," Joe said defiantly.

But as the day wore on and none of their classmates teased them or brought up the subject, the Hardys became convinced that the "ghost" had been serious and not just playing pranks.

"It was no joke," Joe said to Frank on the way home. "If any of the fellows at school had done it, they'd have been kidding us plenty by now."

"Right," Frank agreed. "Joe, do you think the smugglers had anything to do with what happened at the Pollitt place?"

"That's a thought!" exclaimed Joe. "That house on the cliff would be a great hide-out. If the smugglers could make the house appear to be haunted, everyone would stay away."

"I wish Dad would get home, so we could take up this idea with him," Frank said thoughtfully.

But Mr. Hardy did not come home that day. He had often been away for varying lengths of time without sending word, but on this occasion, since he had not taken a bag, the boys felt uneasy.

"Let's not worry Mother about this," Frank said. "But if Dad's not back by Wednesday—at the latest—I think we should do some inquiring. Maybe Pretzel Pete will be able to help us."

Joe agreed. Wednesday was the start of their summer vacation and they could give full time to trying to locate their father.

On Tuesday afternoon the mystery of Mr. Hardy's absence took a strange turn. Frank and Joe came home from school to find their mother seated in the living room, carefully examining a note that she evidently just had received.

"Come here, boys," Mrs. Hardy said in an apprehensive tone. "Look at this and tell me what you think." She handed the note to Frank.

"What is it?" he asked quickly. "Word from Dad?"

"It's supposed to be."

The boys read the note. It was typed on a torn sheet of paper and the signature looked like Fenton Hardy's. It read:

I won't be home for several days. Don't worry. Fenton.

That was all. There was nothing to indicate where the detective was; nothing to show when the note had been written.

"When did you get this, Mother?" asked Frank.

"It came in the afternoon mail. It was addressed to me, and the envelope had a Bayport postmark."

"Why are you worried?" Joe asked. "At least we've heard from Dad."

"But I'm not sure he sent the note."

"What do you mean?"

"Your father and I have an agreement. Whenever he writes me, he puts a secret sign beneath his signature. Fenton was always afraid that someone would forge his name to a letter or note, and perhaps get papers or information that he shouldn't have."

Frank picked up the note again. "There's no sign here. Just Dad's signature."

"It *may* be his signature. If not, it's a very good forgery." Mrs. Hardy was plainly worried.

"If Dad didn't write this note," Joe asked, "who did and why?"

"Your father has many enemies—criminals whom he has been instrumental in sending to prison. If there has been foul play, the note might have been sent to keep us from being suspicious and delay any search."

"Foul play!" exclaimed Frank in alarm. "Then you think something has happened to Dad?"

CHAPTER VII

The Hidden Trail

JOE put an arm around his mother. "Frank and I will start a search for Dad first thing tomorrow," her son said reassuringly.

Next morning, as the boys were dressing, Joe asked, "Where shall we start, Frank?"

"Down at the waterfront. Let's try to find Pretzel Pete and ask him if Dad talked to him on Monday. He may give us a lead."

"Good idea."

The brothers reached the Bayport waterfront early. It was the scene of great activity. A tanker was unloading barrels of oil, and longshoremen were trundling them to waiting trucks.

At another dock a passenger ship was tied up. Porters hurried about, carrying luggage and packages to a line of taxicabs.

Many sailors strolled along the busy street.

Some stepped into restaurants, others into amusement galleries.

"I wonder where Pretzel Pete is," Frank mused. He and Joe had walked four blocks without catching sight of the man.

"Maybe he's not wearing his uniform," Joe surmised. "You know, the one Dad described."

"Let's turn and go back the other way beyond the tanker," Frank suggested.

The boys reversed their direction and made their way through the milling throng for six more blocks.

Suddenly Joe chuckled. "Here comes our man."

Strolling toward them and hawking the product he had for sale came a comical-looking individual. He wore a white cotton suit with a very loose-fitting coat. Around his neck was a vivid red silk handkerchief, embroidered with anchors.

The vendor's trousers had been narrowed at the cuff with bicycle clips to keep them from trailing on the ground, with the result that there was a continuous series of wrinkles from the edge of his coat to his ankles.

The man wore a white hat which came down to his ears. On the wide brown band the name *Pretzel Pete* was embroidered in white letters.

"Boy, that's some gear!" Frank murmured.

Pretzel Pete's garb was bizarre, but he had an

open, honest face. He stopped calling "Pretzels! Hot pretzels! Best in the land!" and smiled at the Hardys. He set down the large metal food warmer he carried. From the top of it rose three short aerials, each ringed with a dozen pretzels.

"You like them hot, or do you prefer them cold?" he asked the brothers.

Joe grinned. "If they're good, I can eat them any way." Then he whispered, "We're Mr. Fenton Hardy's sons. We'd like to talk to you."

At that moment a group of sailors brushed past. Pretzel Pete did not reply until they were out of earshot, then he said to the boys, "Come into this warehouse."

The brothers followed him down the street a short distance and through a doorway into an enormous room which at the moment was practically empty.

"You've brought a message from your pop?" the vendor asked.

Quickly Frank explained to him that their father seemed to be missing. "We thought you might have heard this."

"Yes, I did," Pretzel Pete answered. "But I didn't think nothing about it. I always thought detectives disappeared—sometimes in order to fool people they were after."

"They sometimes do," Joe told him. "But this time seems to be different. Dad said he often came down here to get information from you—because you always give him good tips—and we wondered if you had seen him lately."

"Yes."

"When?"

"Monday morning."

"Dad has been gone ever since."

"Hmm." The man frowned, picked up a pretzel from one of the aerials, and began to munch on it. "Help yourselves, fellows."

Frank and Joe each took one of the pretzels. They had just bitten into the delicious salted rings when Pete continued, "Now you got me worried. Your pop's a fine man and I wouldn't want to see anything happen to him. I'll tell you a place you might look for him."

Pretzel Pete said that he had picked up a bit of information that led him to think an East Indian sailor named Ali Singh might be engaged in some smuggling. The vendor did not know what ship he sailed on, but he understood that the man had come ashore for a secret meeting of some gang.

"This here meeting," Pretzel Pete explained, "was being held out in the country somewhere off the shore road. It was to be in a deserted farmhouse on Hillcrest something or other. I don't remember whether it was 'road' or 'street' or what."

"Was this last Monday?" Frank asked eagerly.

"Oh, no," the vendor answered. "This was about three weeks ago, but when I told your pop he seemed real interested and said he guessed he'd go out there and look around."

Joe broke in, "Dad must have thought the rest of the gang might be living there. Maybe they're holding him a prisoner!"

"Oh, I hope not," Pretzel Pete said worriedly. "But you fellows had better get right out there and take a look."

"We certainly will," Frank told the man.

The brothers thanked Pretzel Pete for the information, then hurried home. Mrs. Hardy was not there, so they did not have a chance to tell her about their plans.

"We'll leave a note," Frank decided and quickly wrote one.

Their hopes high, the brothers set off on their motorcycles on the search for their father. By now they were very familiar with the shore road but did not recall having seen any sign reading Hillcrest.

"Suppose it's not marked," said Joe. "We'll never find it."

Frank gripped his handle bars hard. "If Dad found it, we won't give up until we do."

The motorcycles chugged past side road after side road. The farther away from Bayport the boys went, the farther apart these roads became.

After a while they came to the Kanes' farmhouse and were tempted to stop to see if they might know where Hillcrest was. But just then, a short distance ahead, Joe saw a small car suddenly turn into the shore road. It seemed to have come right out of a clump of bushes and trees.

"Come on, Frank! Let's investigate that place."

The boys pushed ahead, hoping to speak to the driver of the car. But he shot down the road in the opposite direction at terrific speed. When Frank and Joe reached the place from which he had just emerged, they saw that it was a road, though hardly noticeable to anyone passing by.

"I'll take a look and see where it goes," Frank said, shutting off his motorcycle and walking up the grassy, rutted lane. Suddenly he called back, "We're in luck, Joe. I see a homemade sign on a tree. It says Hillcrest Road."

Frank returned to his brother and the boys trundled their machines up among the trees to hide them. Then they set off afoot along the almost impassable woods road.

"There aren't any tire tracks," Joe remarked. "I guess that fellow who drove out of here must have left his car down at the entrance."

Frank nodded, and then in a low tone suggested that they approach the deserted farmhouse very quietly, in case members of the gang were there.

"In fact, I think it might be better if we didn't stay on this road but went through the woods."

Joe agreed and silently the Hardys picked their way along among the trees and through the undergrowth. Five minutes later they came to a clearing in which stood a ramshackle farmhouse. It looked as if it had been abandoned for many years.

The young sleuths stood motionless, observing the run-down building intently. There was not a sound of activity either inside or outside the place. After the boys had waited several minutes, Frank decided to find out whether or not anyone was around. Picking up a large stone, he heaved it with precision aim at the front door. It struck with a resounding thud and dropped to the floor of the sagging porch.

Frank's action brought no response and finally he said to Joe, "I guess nobody's home. Let's look in."

"Right," Joe agreed. "And if Dad's a prisoner there, we'll rescue him!"

The boys walked across the clearing. There was no lock on the door, so they opened it and went inside. The place consisted of only four first-floor rooms. All were empty. A tiny cellar and a loft with a trap door reached by a ladder also proved to have no one in them.

"I don't know whether to be glad or sorry Dad's

not here," said Frank. "It could mean he escaped from the gang if he *was* caught by them and is safely in hiding, but can't send any word to us."

"Or it could mean he's still a captive somewhere else," Joe said. "Let's look around here for clues."

The boys made a systematic search of the place. They found only one item which might prove to be helpful. It was a torn piece of a turkish towel on which the word *Polo* appeared.

"This could have come from some country club where they play polo," Frank figured.

"Or some stable where polo ponies are kept," Joe suggested.

Puzzled, Frank put the scrap in his pocket and the brothers walked down Hillcrest Road. They brought their motorcycles from behind the trees and climbed aboard.

"What do you think we should do next?" Joe asked.

"See Police Chief Collig in Bayport," Frank replied. "I think we should show him this towel. Maybe he can identify it."

Half an hour later they were seated in the chief's office. The tall, burly man took a great interest in the Hardy boys and often worked with Fenton Hardy on his cases. Now Chief Collig gazed at the scrap of toweling for a full minute, then slapped his desk.

"I have it!" he exclaimed. "That's a piece of towel from the *Marco Polo!*"

"What's that?"

"A passenger ship that ties up here once in a while."

Frank and Joe actually jumped in their chairs. Their thoughts went racing to Ali Singh, smugglers, a gang at the deserted farmhouse!

At that moment Chief Collig's phone rang. The Hardys waited politely as he answered, hoping to discuss these new developments with him. But suddenly he put down the instrument, jumped up, and said:

"Emergency, fellows. Have to leave right away!" With that he rushed out of his office.

Frank and Joe arose and disappointedly left headquarters. Returning home, they reported everything to their mother, but upon seeing how forlorn she looked, Frank said hopefully, "That note you received with Dad's name on it *could* have been on the level."

Mrs. Hardy shook her head. "Fenton wouldn't forget the secret sign. I just know he wouldn't."

Word quickly spread through Bayport that the famous Fenton Hardy had disappeared. Early the next morning a thick-set, broad-shouldered young man presented himself at the front door of the Hardy home and said he had something to tell them. Mrs. Hardy invited him to step inside and he stood in the hall, nervously twisting a cap in his hands. As Frank and Joe appeared, the man introduced himself as Sam Bates.

"I'm a truck driver," he told them. "The reason I came around to see you is because I heard you were lookin' for Mr. Hardy. I might be able to help you."

CHAPTER VIII

A Cap on a Peg

"You've seen my father?" Frank asked the truck driver.

"Well, I did see him on Monday," Sam said slowly, "but I don't know where he is now."

"Come in and sit down," Frank urged. "Tell us everything you know."

The four walked to the living room and Mr. Bates sat down uneasily in a large chair.

"Where did you see Mr. Hardy?" Mrs. Hardy asked eagerly.

But Sam Bates was not to be hurried. "I'm a truck driver, see?" he said. "Mostly I drive in Bayport but sometimes I have a run to another town. That's how I come to be out there that mornin'."

"Out where?"

"Along the shore road. I'm sure it was Monday,

because when I came home for supper my wife had been doin' the washin' and she only does that on Monday."

"That was the day Dad left!" Joe exclaimed.

"Well, please go on with the story," Frank prodded Sam Bates. "Where did you see him?"

The truck driver explained that his employer had sent him to a town down the coast to deliver some furniture. "I was about half a mile from the old Pollitt place when I saw a man walkin' along the road. I waved to him, like I always do to people in the country, and then I see it's Mr. Hardy."

"You know my father?" Frank asked.

"Only from his pictures. But I'm sure it was him."

"Dad left here in a sedan," Joe spoke up. "Did you see one around?"

"No, I didn't."

"What was this man wearing?" Mrs. Hardy asked.

"Well, let's see. Dark-brown trousers and a brown-and-black plaid sport jacket. He wasn't wearin' a hat, but I think he had a brown cap in one hand."

Mrs. Hardy's face went white. "Yes, that was my husband." After a moment she added, "Can you tell us anything more?"

"I'm afraid not, ma'am," the trucker said. "You

see, I was in kind of a hurry that mornin', so I didn't notice nothin' else." He arose to leave.

"We certainly thank you for coming to tell us, Mr. Bates," Mrs. Hardy said.

"Yes, you've given us a valuable lead," Frank added. "Now we'll know where to look for Dad."

"I sure hope he shows up," the driver said, walking toward the door. "Let me know if I can help any."

When the man had left, Joe turned to Frank, puzzled. "Do you suppose Dad hid his car and was walking to the Pollitt house? If so, why?"

"Maybe he picked up a clue at that deserted farmhouse on Hillcrest Road," Frank suggested, "and it led to the old Pollitt place. If he left his car somewhere, he must have been planning to investigate the haunted house without being seen."

"Something must have happened to him!" Joe cried out. "Frank, I'll bet he went to Pollitt's and that fake ghost got him. Let's go look for Dad right away!"

But Mrs. Hardy broke in. Her expression was firm. "I don't want you boys to go to that house alone. Maybe you'd just better notify the police and let them make a search."

The brothers looked at each other. Finally Frank, realizing how alarmed she was, said, "Mother, it's possible Dad is there spying on some activities offshore and he's all right but can't leave to phone you. The Pollitt line must have been disconnected. If Joe and I go out there and find him we can bring back a report."

Mrs. Hardy gave a wan smile. "You're very convincing, Frank, when you put it that way. All right. I'll give my permission, but you mustn't go alone."

"Why not, Mother? We can look out for ourselves," Joe insisted.

"Get some of the boys to go with you. There's safety in numbers," his mother said.

The boys agreed to this plan and got busy on the telephone rounding up their pals. Chet Morton and Biff Hooper agreed to go, and they suggested asking Tony Prito and Phil Cohen, two more of the Hardys' friends at Bayport High. Phil owned a motorcycle. He and Tony said they could go along.

Shortly after lunch the group set out. Chet rode with Frank, Biff with Joe, and Tony with Phil. The three motorcycles went out of Bayport, past the Tower Mansion, and along the shore road.

They passed the Kane farmhouse, Hillcrest Road, and at last came in sight of the steep cliff rising from Barmet Bay and crowned by the rambling frame house where Felix Pollitt had lived. All this time they had watched carefully for a sign of Mr. Hardy's car, but found none.

"Your dad hid it well," Chet remarked.

"It's possible someone stole it," Frank told him.

As the boys came closer to the Pollitt property, Phil said to Tony, "Lonely looking place, isn't it?"

"Sure is. Good haunt for a ghost."

When they were still some distance from the lane, Frank, in the lead, brought his motorcycle to a stop and signaled the other two drivers to do likewise.

"What's the matter?" Chet asked.

"We'd better sneak up on the place quietly. If we go any farther and the ghost is there, he'll hear the motorcycles. I vote we leave them here under the trees and go the rest of the way on foot."

The boys hid their machines in a clump of bushes beside the road, and then the six searchers went on toward the lane.

"We'll separate here," Frank decided. "Three of us take one side of the lane and the rest the other side. Keep to the bushes as much as possible, and when we get near the house, lay low for a while and watch the place. When I whistle, you can come out of the bushes and go up to the house."

"That's a good idea," Joe agreed. "Biff, Tony, and I will take the left side of the road."

"Okay."

The boys entered the weeds and undergrowth on either side of the lane. In a few minutes they were lost to view and only an occasional snapping and crackling of branches indicated their presence. The six sleuths crept forward, keeping well in from the lane. After about ten minutes Frank raised his hand as a warning to Chet and Phil. He had caught a glimpse of the house through the dense thicket.

They went on cautiously until they reached the edge of the bushes. From behind the screen of leaves they looked toward the old building. An expression of surprise crossed Frank's face.

"Someone's living here!" he exclaimed in astonishment.

From where the boys stood they hardly recognized the old place. Weeds that had filled the flower beds on their last visit had been completely cleared away. Leaves and twigs had been raked up and the grass cut.

A similar change had been wrought in the house. The hanging shutters had been put in place and the broken library window glass replaced.

"What do you suppose has happened?" Chet whispered.

Frank was puzzled. "Let's wait a minute before we go any farther."

The boys remained at the edge of the bushes, watching the place. A short time later a woman came out of the house carrying a basket of clothes. She walked over to a clothesline stretched between two trees and began to hang up the laundry.

Shortly afterward a man came out, and strode across the yard to a shed where he started filling a basket with logs.

The boys looked at one another in bewilderment. They had expected to find the same sinister and deserted place they had visited previously. Instead, here was a scene of domestic tranquillity.

"There's not much use in our hiding any longer," Frank whispered. "Let's go out and question these people." He gave the prearranged whistle.

The other three boys appeared, and the entire group walked boldly up the lane and across the yard. The man in the woodshed saw them first and straightened up, staring at them with an expression of annoyance. The woman at the clothesline heard their footsteps and turned to face them, her hands on her hips. Her gaunt face wore an unpleasant scowl.

"What do you want?" demanded the man, emerging from the shed.

He was short and thin with close-cropped hair, and he needed a shave. His complexion was swarthy, his eyes narrow under coarse, black brows.

At the same time another man came out of the kitchen and stood on the steps. He was stout and red-haired with a scraggly mustache.

"Yeah, who are you?" he asked.

"We didn't know anyone was living here," Frank explained, edging over to the kitchen door. He wanted to get a look inside the house if possible.

"Well, we're livin' here now," said the red-haired man, "and we don't like snoopers."

"We're not snooping," Frank declared. "We are looking for a man who has disappeared from Bayport."

"Humph!" grunted the woman.

"Why do you think he's around here?" the thin man put in.

"He was last seen in this neighborhood."

"What does he look like?"

"Tall and dark. He was wearing a brown suit and sports jacket and cap."

"There hasn't been anybody around here since we rented this place and moved in," the red-haired man said gruffly.

There seemed to be no prospect of gaining information from the unpleasant trio, so the boys started to leave. But Frank had reached the kitchen door. As he glanced in he gave a start. Hanging on a peg was a brown sports cap!

It looked exactly like the one his father owned, and which he had worn the morning that he had disappeared.

CHAPTER IX

Plan of Attack

"I'm very thirsty," Frank said quickly to the occupants of the Pollitt house. "May I have a drink?"

The red-haired man and the woman looked at each other. They obviously wished to get rid of their visitors as soon as possible. But they could not refuse such a reasonable request.

"Come into the kitchen," said the man grudgingly.

Frank followed him through the door. As he passed the cap he took a good look at it. It *was* his father's, and there were stains on it which looked like blood!

The redheaded man pointed to a sink on the other side of the room. On it stood a plastic cup. "Help yourself," he said gruffly.

Frank went across the room and ran some water from the faucet. As he raised the cup to his lips, his mind was racing. On his way out he glanced again at the peg.

The cap was gone!

Frank gave no sign that he had noticed anything amiss. He walked out into the yard and joined the other five boys.

"I guess we may as well be going," he said nonchalantly.

"You might as well," snapped the woman. "There's no stranger around here, I tell you."

The boys started off down the lane. When they were out of sight of the house, Frank stopped and turned to his companions.

"Do you know what I saw in that kitchen?" he asked tensely.

"What?"

"Dad's cap hanging on a peg!"

"Then he *has* been there!" cried Joe. "They were lying!"

"Yes," Frank continued, "and—and there were bloodstains on the cap!"

"Bloodstains!" Joe exclaimed. "That means he *must* be in trouble. Frank, we've got to go back!"

"We sure do!" his brother agreed. "But I wanted to tell you all about it first."

"What do you think we should do?" Chet asked.

"I'll ask those people in the house about the cap and force a showdown," Frank declared tersely. "We've got to find out where Dad is!"

Resolutely the boys started back to the Pollitt house. When they reached the yard they found the two men and the woman standing by the shed talking earnestly. The woman caught sight of them and spoke warningly to the red-haired man.

"What do you want now?" he demanded, advancing toward the boys.

"We want to know about that sports cap in the kitchen," said Frank firmly.

"What cap? There's no cap in there."

"There isn't now—but there was. It was hanging on a peg when I went in for a drink."

"I don't know anythin' about no cap," persisted the man.

"Perhaps we'd better ask the police to look around," Joe suggested.

The redhead glanced meaningly at the woman. The other man stepped forward. "I know the cap this boy means," he said. "It's mine. What about it?"

"It isn't yours and you know it," Frank declared. "That cap belongs to the man we're looking for."

"I tell you it *is* my cap!" snapped the swarthy man, showing his yellowed teeth in a snarl. "Don't tell me I'm lyin'."

The red-haired man intervened. "You're mistaken, Klein," he said. "I know the cap they mean now. It's the one I found on the road a few days ago."

"Guess you're right, Red," Klein conceded hastily.

"You found it?" asked Frank incredulously.

"Sure, I found it. A brown cap with bloodstains on it."

"That's the one. But why did you hide it when I went into the kitchen?"

"Well, to tell the truth, them bloodstains made me nervous. I didn't know but what there might be some trouble come of it, so I thought I'd better keep that cap out of sight."

"Where did you find it?" Joe asked.

"About a mile from here."

"On the shore road?"

"Yes. It was lyin' right in the middle of the road."

"When was this?"

"A couple of days ago—just after we moved in here."

"Let's see the cap," Chet Morton suggested. "We want to make sure of this."

As Red moved reluctantly toward the kitchen, the woman sniffed. "I don't see why you're makin' all this fuss about an old cap," she said. "Comin' around here disturbin' honest folks."

"We're sorry if we're bothering you," said Joe, "but this is a very serious matter."

Red came out of the house holding the cap. He tossed it to Frank.

The boy turned back the inside flap and there he found what he was looking for—the initials F. H. printed in gold on the leather band.

"It's Dad's cap all right."

"I don't like the look of those bloodstains," said Joe in a low voice. "He must have been badly hurt."

"Are you sure you found this on the road?" Frank asked, still suspicious.

"You don't think I'd lie about it, do you?" Red answered belligerently.

"I can't contradict you, but I'm going to turn this over to the police," Frank told him. "If you know anything more about it, you'd better speak up now."

"He doesn't know anything about it," shrilled the woman angrily. "Go away and don't bother us. Didn't he tell you he found the cap on the road? I told him to burn up the dirty thing. But he wanted to have it cleaned and wear it."

The boys turned away, Frank still holding the cap. "Come on, fellows," he said. "Let's get out of here."

As the boys started down the lane they cast a last glance back at the yard. The woman and the two men were standing just where the young sleuths had left them. The woman was motionless, her hands on her hips. Red was standing with his arms folded, and Klein, the swarthy man, was lean-

"He doesn't know anything about the cap,"
the woman shrilled

ing against a tree. All three were gazing intently and silently after the departing boys.

"I'm sure that those people know more about Dad's cap than they're telling," Frank said grimly, as the boys mounted their motorcycles and rode back toward Bayport.

"What are you planning to do next?" Phil asked as he pulled his machine alongside Frank's.

"I'm going right to Chief Collig and tell him the whole story."

"Okay, we're with you!"

The boys rode directly to police headquarters and left their motorcycles in the parking lot. Chief Collig looked up as his six visitors were ushered into his office.

"Well," he said heartily, "this is quite a delegation! What can I do for you?"

As Frank and Joe took turns, with an occasional graphic illustration from one of the other boys, they told the full story and showed him the blood-stained cap.

Chief Collig looked grave. "I don't like the sound of this at all," he said finally. "We must find your father at once! This cap is a good clue." Then he went on, "Of course you realize that the area where the Pollitt house is located is outside the limits of Bayport, so my men can't go there. But I'll get in touch with Captain Ryder of the State Police at once, so he can assign men to the case."

The boys thanked the chief for his help and left. Chet, Tony, Biff, and Phil went their separate ways while Frank and Joe turned toward home. They decided not to upset their mother about the bloodstained cap, but merely tell her that the State Police would take over the search for her husband.

"I still think there's some connection between Dad's disappearance and the smuggling outfit and the house on the cliff," Frank declared.

"What I've been wondering," said Joe, "is where those two motorboats came from that day Jones was attacked. We didn't see them out in the ocean earlier—at least not both of them."

"That's right. They could have come right out from under the cliff."

"You mean, Frank, there might be a secret harbor in there?"

"Might be. Here's the way it could work. Dad suspects smugglers are operating in this territory from a base that he has been unable to find." Frank spread his arms. "The base is the old Pollitt place! What more do you want?"

"But the house is on top of a *cliff*."

"There could be a secret passage from the house to a hidden harbor at the foot of the cliff."

"Good night, Frank, it sure sounds reasonable!"

"And perhaps that explains why the kidnapers got away with Jones so quickly on Saturday. If

they left the Kane farmhouse just a little while before we did, we should have been able to get within
sight of their car. But we didn't."

"You mean they turned in at the Pollitt place?"

"Why not? Probably Jones is hidden there right
now."

"And maybe Dad too," Joe cried out excitedly.

"That's right. I'm against just sitting and waiting for the state troopers to find him. How about
asking Tony if he will lend us his motorboat, so
we can investigate the foot of that cliff?"

"I get you!" Joe agreed enthusiastically. "And if
we pick up any information we can turn it over to
the State Police and they can raid the Pollitt
place!"

CHAPTER X

A Watery Tunnel

WHEN the brothers arrived home Frank and Joe assured their mother that the State Police would soon find Mr. Hardy. Some of the anxiety left her face as she listened to her sons' reassuring words.

When she went to the kitchen to start preparations for supper, the boys went to phone Tony Prito. After Frank explained their plan to him, he agreed at once to let them use the *Napoli*, provided they took him along.

"I wouldn't miss it for anything," he said. "But I can't go until afternoon. Have to do some work for my dad in the morning. I'll meet you at the boathouse at two o'clock."

"Swell, Tony. I have a job of my own in the morning."

Chet called a few minutes later. As Frank finished telling him about the plan, he whistled.

"You fellows have got your nerve all right. But count me in, will you? I started this thing with you and I'd like to finish it. We've got to find your father!"

After Chet had said good-by, Joe asked his brother, "What's on for the morning?"

"I want to go down to the waterfront and talk to Pretzel Pete again. He might have another clue. Also, I want to find out when the *Marco Polo* is due back here."

Joe nodded. "I get it. You think something may be going on then?"

"Right. And if we can find Dad and lead the Coast Guard to the smugglers before the boat docks—"

"Brother, that's a big order."

By nine o'clock the following morning Frank and Joe were down at the Bayport docks. Pretzel Pete was not in evidence.

"We'd better be cagey about asking when the *Marco Polo's* coming in," Frank cautioned. "The smugglers probably have spies around here and we'd sure be targets."

Acting as if there were no problems on their minds, Frank and Joe strolled along whistling. Once they joined a group of people who were watching a sidewalk merchant. The man was demonstrating little jumping animals. Frank and Joe laughed as they bought a monkey and a kangaroo. "Iola and Callie will get a kick out of these," Joe predicted.

"Say, Frank, here comes Pretzel Pete now!" Joe whispered.

The Hardys went up the street, saying in a loud voice in case anyone was listening, that they were hungry and glad to see Pete.

"Nobody can make pretzels like yours," Joe exclaimed. "Give me a dozen. Two for my mouth and ten for my pockets."

As Pretzel Pete laughed and pulled out a cellophane bag to fill the order, Frank said in a whisper, "Heard anything new?"

"Not a thing, son." Pete could talk without moving his lips. "But I may know something tomorrow."

"How come?"

"The *Marco Polo's* docking real early—five A.M. I heard Ali Singh is one of the crew. I'll try to get a line on him."

"Great! We'll be seeing you."

The boys moved off, and to avoid arousing any suspicion as to why they were in the area, headed for a famous fish market.

"Mother will be surprised to see our morning's catch," Joe said with a grin as he picked out a large bluefish.

The brothers did not discuss the exciting information Pretzel Pete had given them until they were in the safety of their own home. Then Joe burst out, "Frank, if the *Marco Polo* gets offshore during the night, it'll have to lay outside until it's time to dock!"

"And that'll give those smugglers a real break in picking up the stolen drugs!" Frank added. "Maybe we should pass along our suspicions to the Coast Guard."

"Not yet," Joe objected. "All we have to go on is Pretzel Pete's statements about Ali Singh. Maybe we'll learn more this afternoon and then we can report it."

"I guess you're right," Frank concluded. "If those smugglers are holding Dad, and find out that we've tipped off the Coast Guard, they'll certainly harm him."

"You have a point."

When Frank and Joe reached the Prito boat-house at two o'clock, Tony and Chet were already there. Tony was tuning up the motor, which purred evenly.

"No word from your dad yet?" Tony asked. The Hardys shook their heads as they stepped aboard.

The *Napoli* was a rangy, powerful craft with graceful lines and was the pride of Tony's life. The boat moved slowly out into the waters of Barmet Bay and then gathered speed as it headed toward the ocean.

"Rough water," Frank remarked as breaking

swells hit the hull. Salt spray dashed over the bow
of the *Napoli* as it plunged on through the white-
caps. Bayport soon became a speck nestled at the
curve of the horseshoe-shaped body of water.
Reaching the ocean, Tony turned north. The boys
could see the white line of the shore road rising
and falling along the coast. Soon they passed the
Kane farm. Two miles farther on they came within
sight of the cliff upon which the Pollitt house
stood. It looked stark and forbidding above the
rocks, its roof and chimneys silhouetted against
the sky.

"Pretty steep cliff," Tony observed. "I can't see
how anyone could make his way up and down that
slope to get to the house."

"That's probably why nobody has suspected the
place of being a smuggling base," Frank replied.
"But perhaps when we look around we'll find an
answer."

Tony steered the boat closer toward the shore,
so that it would not be visible from the Pollitt
grounds. Then he slackened speed in order that
the sound of the engine would be less noticeable,
and the craft made its way toward the bottom of
the cliff.

There were currents here that demanded skill-
ful navigation, but Tony brought the *Napoli*
through them easily, and at last the boat was chug-
ging along close to the face of the cliff.

The boys eagerly scanned the formidable wall of rock. It was scarred and seamed and the base had been eaten away by the incessant battering of waves. There was no indication of a path.

Suddenly Tony turned the wheel sharply. The *Napoli* swerved swiftly to one side. He gave it power and the craft leaped forward with a roar.

"What's the matter?" Frank asked in alarm.

Tony gazed straight ahead, tense and alert. Another shift of the wheel and the *Napoli* swerved again.

Then Chet and the Hardys saw the danger. There were rocks at the base of the cliff. One of them, black and sharp, like an ugly tooth, jutted out of the water almost at the boat's side. Only Tony's quick eye had saved the *Napoli* from hitting it!

They had blundered into a veritable maze of reefs which extended for several yards ahead. Tony's passengers held their breaths. It seemed impossible that they could run the gantlet of those rocks without tearing out the bottom of the craft.

But luck was with them. The *Napoli* dodged the last dangerous rock, and shot forward into open water.

Tony sank back with a sigh of relief. "Whew, that was close!" he exclaimed. "I didn't see those rocks until we were right on top of them. If we'd ever struck one of them we'd have been goners."

Frank, Joe, and Chet nodded in solemn agreement. Then, suddenly, Frank cried out, "Turn back! I think I saw an opening!"

Tony swung the boat around. The opening which Frank had spotted was a long, narrow tunnel. It led right through the cliff!

"This might be the secret entrance!" Joe exclaimed.

"I think it's large enough for the boat to go through," said Tony. "Want me to try it?"

Frank nodded tensely. "Go ahead."

The *Napoli* slipped through the opening and in a few moments came out into a pond of considerable extent. The boys looked about expectantly. Steep slopes covered with scraggly trees and bushes reached to the water's edge. But there was no path or indication that any human being ever came down to the pond.

Suddenly Frank gave a gasp of surprise and said, "Look to my right, fellows."

Among the thickets at the base of the steepest slope stood a man. He was very tall, his face was weather-beaten, and his lips thin and cruel. He stood quietly, looking at the boys without a shadow of expression on his sinister face.

Upon realizing he had been observed, the man shouted, "Get out of here!"

Tony throttled the engine and Frank called, "We aren't doing any harm."

"I said 'Get out!' This is private property."

The boys hesitated. Instantly the man, as though to back up his commands, reached significantly toward the holster of a revolver.

"Turn that boat around and beat it!" he snapped. "And don't ever come back here! Not if you know what's good for you."

The boys realized that nothing would be gained by argument. Tony slowly brought the boat around.

"Okay," Joe called cheerfully.

The stranger did not reply. He stood gazing fixedly after them, his left hand pointing to the exit, his right tapping the gun holster, as the motorboat made its way out through the tunnel.

"Looks as if he didn't want us around," remarked Tony facetiously, as soon as the *Napoli* was in open water again.

"He sure didn't!" Frank exclaimed. "I expected him to start popping that gun at any moment!"

"He must have an important reason. Who and what do you suppose he is?" Tony asked in bewilderment.

"Fellows," Frank said thoughtfully, "I think that man might have been Snattman!"

CHAPTER XI

Cliff Watchers

"FRANK!" Joe exclaimed. "I think you've hit it! That man had no reason to act the way he did unless he's covering up something."

"Something like smuggling, you mean," said Chet. "He must be Snattman or one of his gang."

"And," Frank went on, "the fact that he was in that cove must mean he has some connection with the house on the cliff."

"Snattman, king of the smugglers!" Tony whistled. "You guys really get in some interesting situations!"

"I'll bet that he's one of the fellows who chased Jones that day in the motorboat," Joe cried.

"And tried to kill him," Frank continued the thought.

"Let's get away from here!" Chet urged.

"Why should we go now?" Frank demanded.

"We've stumbled on something important. That hidden pond may be the smugglers' base."

"But if they use the house how do they get to it?" Tony asked. "Those cliffs up from the pond were mighty steep."

"There must be some other way that we couldn't see," Joe said. "What say we hang around here for a while and find out what we can?"

Tony caught the Hardys' enthusiasm and agreed to keep the motorboat in the vicinity of the cliff.

"That fellow may be keeping his eye on us and we don't want him to know that we're watching the place," Frank observed. "Let's run back to the bay and cruise up and down a while, then return."

Chet sighed. "I'm glad none of you argued with that armed man."

"Right," Joe replied. "As it is, he must think we were simply out for a cruise and wandered into that tunnel by mistake."

"Yes," his brother agreed. "If he'd known we're hunting for Dad, he might have acted very differently."

In the late afternoon Tony took the *Napoli* back to the suspected shore spot. Keeping well out from the breaking waves, he cruised along the cliff. The boys kept a sharp eye on the location of the tunnel. As the boat passed it they were just able to distinguish the narrow opening in the rocks.

"I won't be able to go in there after a while," Tony remarked. "The tide's coming in. At high tide I'll bet that tunnel is filled with water."

Suddenly Tony swung his craft so hard to the right that the other boys lost their balance.

"Sorry, fellows," he said. "Saw a log—oh!"

He shut off his engine in a flash and leaned over the gunwale. His companions picked themselves up and asked what had happened.

"Propeller started to foul up with some wire on that log." Tony began to peel off his clothes. "Get me some pliers, will you?"

Frank opened a locker and found a pair. Taking them, Tony dived overboard. A minute later he reappeared and climbed in. "I'm lucky," he said. "Just plain lucky. Two seconds more and all that wire would have been wound around the prop and the log would have knocked it off."

"Good night!" Chet exclaimed. "It would have been a long swim home."

Joe slapped Tony on the back. "Good work, boy. I'd hate to see the *Napoli* out of commission."

Chet and Frank hauled the log aboard, so it would not damage any other craft. "This is a fence post with barbed wire!" Chet said. "Wowee! It's good you spotted that log, Tony."

Tony dressed, then started the engine. He

cruised around for more than an hour, but the boys saw no sign of life about the base of the cliff. They could see the Pollitt house, but to their amazement no lights appeared in it as twilight came.

"How much longer do you think we should stay out here?" Chet asked. "I'm getting hungry."

"I have a few pretzels and a candy bar, but that's not much for four of us," Joe remarked.

"Aha!" crowed Tony. "I have a surprise for you! I stowed away a little food before we took off." With that he pulled a paper bag from the locker and passed each boy a large sandwich, a piece of chocolate cake, and a bottle of lemon soda.

"You deserve a medal," Chet remarked as he bit into a layer of ham and cheese.

"You sure do!" Frank agreed. "I think we should stay right here for a while and watch. It's my guess the smugglers will be on the job tonight. Don't forget that the *Marco Polo* is docking tomorrow morning."

"I get it," said Chet. "If she lays offshore or steams in slowly, it'll give Ali Singh a chance to drop the stolen drugs overboard to Snattman."

"Correct," said Frank.

Tony looked intently at the Hardys. "Is it your idea to keep Snattman from meeting Ali Singh? But what about your father? I thought we came out here to get a line on how to rescue him."

The brothers exchanged glances, then Joe said, "Of course that's our main purpose, but we hope that we can do both."

Twilight deepened into darkness and lights could be seen here and there through the haze. The cliff was only a black smudge and the house above was still unlighted.

Suddenly the boys heard a muffled sound. Tony slowed the *Napoli* and they listened intently.

"Another motorboat," Tony whispered.

The sound seemed to come from near the cliff. Straining their eyes in that direction, the four were at last able to distinguish a faint moving light.

"Can you head over that way, Tony?" Frank asked in a low voice. "And could you take a chance on turning off our lights?"

"Sure. Here goes. The wind's blowing from the land, so our engine won't be heard from the shore."

The boys were tense with excitement as the *Napoli* moved slowly toward the light. As the boat crept nearer the cliff, they could barely distinguish the outline of a motorboat. The craft seemed to be making its way carefully out of the very face of the cliff.

"It must have come from that tunnel!" Joe whispered to Frank.

"Yes."

The *Napoli* went closer, in imminent danger of being discovered or of being washed ashore onto the rocks. Finally the other boat slowed to a crawl. Then came the faint clatter of oars and low voices. The motorboat had evidently met a rowboat.

The next moment, with an abrupt roar, the motorboat turned and raced out to sea at an ever-increasing rate of speed.

"Where can it be going?" said Tony, in amazement. "Out to meet the *Marco Polo?*"

"Probably," Frank replied, "and we'd never catch it. I wonder where the rowboat's going."

The four boys waited in silence for several minutes. Then the rattle of oars came again. This time the sound was closer. The rowboat was coming toward them!

"What'll we do now?" Tony asked.

"Turn off your engine," Frank whispered. Tony complied.

Through the gloom suddenly came snatches of conversation from the rowboat. "—a hundred pounds—" they heard a man say harshly, and then the rest of the sentence was lost. There was a lengthy murmur of voices, then, "I don't know. It's risky—"

The wind died down just then and two voices could be heard distinctly. "Ali Singh's share—" one man was saying.

"That's right. We can't forget him," the gruff voice replied.

"I hope they get away all right."

"What are you worryin' about? Of course they'll get away."

"We've been spotted, you know."

"It's all your imagination. Nobody suspects."

"Those boys at the house—"

"Just dumb kids. If they come nosin' around again, we'll knock 'em on the head."

"I don't like this rough stuff. It's dangerous."

"We've got to do it or we'll end up in the pen. What's the matter with you tonight? You're nervous."

"I'm worried. I've got a hunch we'd better clear out of here."

"Clear out!" replied the other contemptuously. "Are you crazy? Why, this place is as safe as a church." The man laughed sardonically. "Haven't we got all the squealers locked up? And tonight we make the big cleanup and get away."

"Well, maybe you're right," said the first man doubtfully. "But still—"

His voice died away as the boat entered the tunnel.

Joe grabbed Frank's arm. "Did you hear that? All the squealers locked up? I'll bet Dad's one of them and he's a prisoner somewhere around here."

"And this is the hide-out of Snattman and

the other smugglers he was after," Frank added.

"I don't like this," Chet spoke up. "Let's leave here and get the police."

Frank shook his head. "It would take so long we might goof the whole thing. Tell you what. Joe and I will follow that rowboat through the tunnel!"

"How?"

"On foot or swim. I don't think it's deep along the edges."

"You mean Chet and I will wait here?" Tony asked.

"No," Frank answered. "You two beat it back to Bayport and notify the Coast Guard. Tell them we're on the track of smugglers and ask them to send some men here."

"And tell them our suspicions about Ali Singh and the *Marco Polo*," Joe added. "They can radio the captain to keep an eye on him."

"Okay," said Tony. "I'll do that. First I'll put you ashore."

"Don't go too close or you'll hit those rocks and wreck the boat," Frank warned. "Joe and I can swim to shore. Then we'll work around into the tunnel and see what we can find. If we do discover anything, we'll wait at the entrance and show the men from the Coast Guard where to go when they get here."

Tony edged the boat in as close to the dark

shore as he dared without lights. Quickly Frank and Joe took off their slacks, T shirts, sweaters, and sneakers. They rolled them up, and with twine which Tony provided, tied the bundles on top of their heads. Then they slipped over the side into the water. The *Napoli* sped off.

Frank and Joe were only a few yards from the rocks and after a short swim emerged on the mainland.

"Well, here goes!" Joe whispered, heading for the tunnel.

CHAPTER XII

The Secret Passage

CAUTIOUSLY Frank and Joe made their way across the slippery rocks. Suddenly there was a loud splash as Joe lost his footing.

"Are you all right?" Frank whispered, as he came up to where his brother was standing in the shallow water at the edge of the cliff.

"Yes. For a moment I sure thought I'd sprained my ankle," Joe replied tensely, "but it seems to be okay now."

"Give me your hand," Frank whispered and quickly pulled Joe back onto the rocks.

The Hardys had landed at a point some twenty-five yards from the tunnel opening, but the climb over the treacherous rocks was so difficult that the distance seemed much longer. It was very dark in the shadow of the steep cliff. The waves breaking against the rocks had a lonely and foreboding sound.

"Good night!" Joe muttered. "Aren't we ever coming to that tunnel?"

"Take it easy," Frank advised. "It can't be much farther."

"I hope Tony and Chet will hurry back with help," Joe said. "This is a ticklish job."

"If anybody's on guard here, we'll certainly be at a disadvantage," Frank remarked in a barely audible tone. "Watch out!"

By this time they had reached the entrance to the tunnel. After a few cautious steps they discovered that the narrow piece of land between the water and the base of the cliff was covered by a thick growth of bushes.

Frank turned to Joe. "If we try to walk through all that stuff," he whispered, "we're sure to be heard. That is, if those men are in here some place."

Joe grunted in agreement. "What shall we do?"

Tentatively, Frank put one foot into the water from the rock on which he was standing.

"It isn't deep," he said. "I guess we can wade through."

The boys hugged the wall and started off. Fortunately, the water came only to their knees because there was a shelf of rocks all the way along. The brothers' hearts beat wildly. What would they find ahead of them?

The boys had not heard a sound since entering

the tunnel. It appeared that the men in the rowboat had gone on to some secret hiding place.

"I think I'll risk my flashlight," Frank said in a low voice as they reached the pond. "We can't find out anything without it."

He pulled one he always carried from its waterproof case and snapped it on. The yellow beam shone over the pond. There was no sign of the rowboat.

"How do you think those men got out of here?" Joe asked. "Do you suppose there's another opening?"

Frank turned the flashlight onto the steep sides surrounding the water. "I don't see any. My guess is that those men hid the boat some place. Let's make a thorough search."

Slowly the brothers began to walk around the edge of the pond, brushing aside the heavy growth and peering among the bushes. They had about given up in despair as they reached the section by the far wall of the tunnel. Then, as Frank beamed the flashlight over the thicket, he exclaimed hoarsely, "Look!"

"A door!" Joe whispered tensely.

The door had been so cleverly concealed that it would not have been seen in full daylight except at close quarters. The glare of the flashlight, however, brought the artificial screen of branches and leaves into sharp relief against the dark cliffside.

"This explains it," Joe said. "The men in the boat went through here. I wonder where it goes."

In order to avoid detection, Frank extinguished his light before trying to open the door. He swung it open inch by inch, half expecting to find lights and people beyond. But there was only darkness. Luckily the door had made no noise. Frank turned on his light again.

Ahead was a watery passageway some ten feet wide and twenty-five feet long, with a ledge running along one side. At the end was a tiny wharf with a rowboat tied to a post.

"This is fantastic!" Joe whispered. "And it must have been here a long time. Do you suppose it's connected with the Pollitt place?"

"If it is, it could mean old Mr. Pollitt was mixed up with the smugglers!" Frank answered. "Hey, do you suppose Snattman is his nephew?"

Excited over this possible new angle to the case, Frank and Joe stepped onto the ledge. They dressed, then quietly inched forward. Reaching the wharf, they looked about them as Frank beamed his flashlight on the walls.

"Hold it!" Joe whispered.

Directly ahead was a crude arch in the rock. Beyond it, the boys could see a steep flight of stone steps. Their hearts pounded with excitement.

"We've found it!" Frank whispered. "This must be the secret passageway!"

"Yes," Joe agreed, "and from the distance we've come I'd figure that we're right underneath the house on the cliff."

"Let's go up."

The light cast strange shadows in the passage through the rocks. Water dripped from the walls. The boys tiptoed forward and stealthily began the ascent.

As they crept up the stairs, Frank flashed the light ahead of them. Shortly they could see that the steps ended at a heavy door. Its framework was set into the wall of rock. Above them was only a rocky ceiling.

When Frank and Joe reached the door, they hesitated. Both were thinking, "If we go through that door and find the gang of smugglers, we'll never get out. But, on the other hand, we *must* find Dad!"

Frank stepped forward, pressed his ear against the door, and listened intently. There was not a sound beyond.

He turned off his light and looked carefully around the sides of the door to see if he could catch a glimmer of any illumination from the other side. There was only darkness.

"I guess there's no one inside," he said to Joe. "Let's see if we can open it."

Frank felt for the latch. The door did not move. "It must be locked," he whispered.

"Try it again. Maybe it's just stuck."

Frank put his hand on the latch, this time also pushing the door with his shoulder. Suddenly, with a noise which echoed from wall to wall, the latch snapped and the door swung open.

Joe stepped forward, but Frank put out a restraining hand. "Wait!" he cautioned. "That noise may bring someone."

Tensely, they stood alert for the slightest sound. But none came. Hopeful that there was no one in the area beyond, Frank switched on the flashlight.

The vivid beam cut the darkness and revealed a gloomy cave hewn out of the rock in the very center of the cliff. The boys wondered if it had been a natural cave. It was filled with boxes, bales, and packages distributed about the floor and piled against the walls.

"Smuggled goods!" Frank and Joe thought.

The fact that the majority of the boxes bore labels of foreign countries seemed to verify their suspicions.

Convinced that the cave was unoccupied, the boys stepped through the doorway and looked about for another door or opening. They saw none. Was this the end of the trail?

"But it couldn't be," the young sleuths thought. "Those men went *some* place."

Bolts of beautiful silk had been tossed on top

of some of the bales. Valuable tapestries were also lying carelessly around. In one corner four boxes were piled on top of one another. Frank accidentally knocked the flashlight against one of these and it gave forth a hollow sound.

"It's empty," he whispered.

An idea struck him that perhaps these boxes had been piled up to conceal some passage leading out of the secret storeroom. He mentioned his suspicion to Joe.

"But how could the men pile the boxes up there after they went out?" his brother questioned.

"This gang is smart enough for anything. Let's move these boxes away and maybe we'll find out."

Frank seized the topmost box. It was very light and he removed it from the pile without difficulty.

"I thought so!" Frank said with satisfaction. The flashlight had revealed the top of a door which had been hidden from view.

The boys lost no time in moving the other three boxes. Then Frank and Joe discovered how it was possible for the boxes to be piled up in such a position, in spite of the fact that the smugglers had left the cave and closed the door behind them.

Attached to the bottom of the door was a thin

wooden platform that projected out over the floor of the cave and on this the boxes had been piled.

"Very clever," Joe remarked. "Whenever any one leaves the cave and closes the door, the boxes swing in with the platform and it looks as though they were piled up on the floor."

"Right. Well, let's see where the door leads," Frank proposed.

He snapped off his light and with utmost caution opened the door. It made no sound. Again there was darkness ahead.

"What a maze!" Frank whispered as he turned on his flash and beamed the light ahead.

Another stone-lined passage with a flight of steps at the end!

Suddenly Frank stiffened and laid a warning hand on his brother's arm. "Voices!" he said in a low tone and snapped off his light.

The boys listened intently. They could hear a man's voice in the distance. Neither could distinguish what he was saying, for he was still too far away, but gradually the tones grew louder. Then, to the brothers' alarm, they heard footsteps. Hastily they retreated into the secret cave.

"Quick! The door!" Frank urged.

They closed it quietly.

"Now the boxes. If those men come in here

they'll notice that the boxes have been moved!"
He turned on the light but shielded it with his
hand.

Swiftly Joe piled the empty boxes back onto the
platform that projected from the bottom of the
door. He worked as silently and quickly as possible,
but could hear the footsteps drawing closer and
closer.

Finally the topmost box was in place.

"Out the other door!" Frank hissed into Joe's
ear.

They sped across the floor of the cave toward
the door opening onto the stairs they had recently
ascended. But hardly had they reached it before
they heard a rattle at the latch of the door on the
opposite side of the cave.

"We haven't time," Frank whispered. "Hide!"

The beam of the flashlight revealed a number
of boxes close to the door. On top of these someone had thrown a heavy bolt of silk, the folds of
which hung down to the floor. The brothers
scrambled swiftly behind the boxes, pressing
themselves close against the wall. They had just
enough time to hide and switch out Frank's light
before they heard the other door open.

"There's a bunch of drugs in that shipment that
came in three weeks ago," they heard a husky
voice say. "We'll take it upstairs. Burke says he
can get rid of it for us right away. No use leaving

it down here. Got to make room for the new shipment."

"Right," the Hardys heard someone else reply.
"Anything else to go up?"

"No. I'll switch on the light."

There was a click, and suddenly the cave was
flooded with light. It had been wired for elec-
tricity.

Frank and Joe crouched in their hiding place,
holding their breaths in terror. Would they be
discovered?

Footsteps slowly approached the boxes behind
which they were concealed!

CHAPTER XIII

A Startling Discovery

FRANK AND JOE tried to crowd themselves into the smallest space possible as the men came nearer to their hiding place. The electric light bulb hanging from the center of the ceiling cast such a strong illumination over the cave that the boys felt certain they would be discovered.

The boxes were placed a small distance apart, and only the fact that folds of silk hung down over the open spaces between the boxes prevented the boys from being seen immediately. However, through a crack in one of the crates, the Hardys could just make out two husky-looking figures.

"Here's some o' that Japanese silk," the boys heard one of the men say. "I'd better take a bolt of that up too. Burke said he could place some more of it."

Instantly the same thought ran through both

the brothers' minds. If the man picked up the silk, they would surely be found!

"Don't be crazy!" the other man objected. "You know you won't get any credit for pushin' a sale. Why break your arm luggin' all that stuff upstairs?"

"Well," the first man explained in a whining tone, "I thought maybe we could get rid of some more of this swag and make ourselves a little extra dough."

"Naw," his companion snarled. "I can tell you ain't been with this gang long. You never get any thanks around here for thinkin'. If Burke don't take the extra stuff, the boss'll make you bring it all the way down again."

"Maybe you're right."

"Sure I'm right! My idea for the rest of us in this gang is to do just what Snattman tells us to and no more."

"You got somethin' there, Bud. Okay. We'll just take up the package of drugs and leave the rest."

To the boys' relief the men turned away and went over to the other side of the room. Frank and Joe did not dare peer out, but they could hear the sound of boxes being shifted.

Then came the words, "All set. I've got the packages. Let's go!"

The switch was snapped and the cave was

plunged into darkness. The Hardys began to breathe normally again. The door to the corridor closed and faintly the boys could detect the men's footsteps as they ascended the stairs at the end of it.

When they had died away completely, Frank switched on the flashlight. "Wow!" he said, giving a tremendous sigh of relief. "That was a close call! I sure thought they had us."

"Me too," Joe agreed. "We wouldn't have had a chance with that pair. Looked like a couple of wrestlers."

"Do we dare follow them?"

"You bet. I'd say we've solved the smuggling mystery, but we've still got to find out if they're holding Dad," Joe said grimly.

"We'll have to watch our step even more carefully. We don't want to walk right into the whole ring of smugglers," Frank reminded him.

"Right. I don't crave anything worse than what we've just gone through," said Joe. "I thought I'd die of suspense while that pair was in here."

They crossed the room, opened the door, and started up the dark passageway. Presently they were confronted by the flight of steps. Part way up there was a landing, then more steps with a door at the top.

"I'll go first," Frank offered. "Stick close behind me. I think I'll keep the flash off."

"That's right," Joe agreed. "Snattman might

have a guard at the top and there's no use advertising our presence."

Step by step, the boys crept upward in the inky blackness. Then they found themselves on a crude landing of planks. Carefully they felt their way along the side of the rock wall until they reached the next flight of steps.

Here the brothers stopped again to listen. Silence.

"So far, so good," Frank whispered. "But somehow I don't like this whole thing. I have a feeling we're walking into a trap."

"We can't quit now," Joe answered. "But I admit I'm scared."

Still groping in the dark, the boys climbed up and up until they were nearly winded.

"Where are we?" Joe panted. "I feel as if I've been climbing stairs for an hour!"

"Me too," Frank agreed. "The cliff doesn't look this high from the outside."

They rested a minute, then continued their journey. Groping around, they finally reached another door. Frank hunted for the door handle. Finding it, he turned the knob ever so slightly to find out if the door was locked.

"I can open it," Frank said in Joe's ear, "but we'd better wait a few minutes."

"Every second is vital if Dad's a prisoner," Joe objected.

Frank was about to accede to his brother's urging when both boys heard footsteps on the other side of the door. A chill ran down their spines.

"Shall we run?" Joe said fearfully.

"It wouldn't do us any good. Listen!"

There came a queer shuffling sound and a sigh from somewhere beyond the door. That was all.

"Someone's in there," Frank breathed. Joe nodded in the darkness.

The boys did not know what to do. The gang might have posted a sentry. If there was only one, the Hardys might be able to jump the man and disarm him. However, they probably could not do it without making some noise and attracting the attention of the rest of the smugglers.

Frank and Joe gritted their teeth. They couldn't give up now!

As they were trying to decide how to proceed, the situation took an unexpected turn. A door slammed in the distance. Then came the murmur of voices and the sound of advancing footsteps.

"This nonsense has gone far enough," a man said angrily. "He'll write that note at once, or I'll know the reason why."

The boys started. The voice was that of the man who had ordered them to leave the pond during the afternoon.

"That's right, chief!" another voice spoke up.

"Make him do as you say and get the heat off us until we've got all the loot moved."

"If he doesn't write it, he'll never get out of here alive," the first man promised coldly.

Instantly Frank and Joe thought of the note their mother had received. Was the man these smugglers were talking about their father? Or was he someone else—maybe Jones, who was to be forced to obey them or perhaps lose his life?

The speakers went a short distance beyond the door behind which Frank and Joe were standing. Then they heard the click of a switch. A faint beam of yellow light shone beneath the door. The brothers figured there was a corridor beyond and three or four men had entered a room opening from it.

"Well, I see you're still here," said the man who had been addressed as chief. "You'll find this an easier place to get into than out of."

A weary voice answered him. The tones were low, so the boys pressed closer to the door. But try as they might, they could not distinguish the words.

"You're a prisoner here and you'll stay here until you die unless you write that note."

Again the weary voice spoke, but the tones were still so indistinct that the boys could not hear the answer.

"You won't write it, eh? We'll see what we can do to persuade you."

"Let him go hungry for a few days. That'll persuade him!" put in one of the other men. This brought a hoarse laugh from his companions.

"You'll be hungry enough if you don't write that letter," the chief agreed. "Are you going to write it?"

"No," the boys barely heard the prisoner answer.

The chief said sourly, "You've got too much on us. We can't afford to let you go now. But if you write that letter, we'll leave you some food, so that you won't starve. You'll break out eventually, but not in time to do us any harm. Well, what do you say? Want some food?"

There was no reply from the prisoner.

"Give his arm a little twist," suggested one of the smugglers.

At this the Hardys' blood boiled with rage. Their first impulse was to fling open the door and rush to the aid of the person who was being tormented. But they realized they were helpless against so many men. Their only hope lay in the arrival of the Coast Guard men, but they might come too late!

"Chief, shall I give this guy the works?" one of the smugglers asked.

"No," the leader answered quickly. "None of

that rough stuff. We'll do it the easy way—starvation. I'm giving him one more chance. He can write that note now or we'll leave him here to starve when we make our getaway."

Still there was no reply.

To Frank's and Joe's ears came a scraping sound as if a chair was being moved forward.

"You won't talk, eh?" The leader's voice grew ugly.

There was a pause of a few seconds, then suddenly he shouted, "Write that note, Hardy, or you'll be sorry—as sure as my name's Snattman!"

CHAPTER XIV

Captured

JOE gave a start. "It *is* Dad!" he whispered hoarsely. "He found the smugglers' hide-out!"

Frank nudged his brother warningly. "Not so loud."

The boys' worst fears were realized—their father was not only a prisoner of the smugglers, but also his life was being threatened!

"Write that note!" Snattman demanded.

"I won't write it," Fenton Hardy replied in a weak but clear voice.

The chief persisted. "You heard what I said. Write it or be left here to starve."

"I'll starve."

"You'll change your mind in a day or two. You think you're hungry now, but wait until we cut off your food entirely. Then you'll see. You'll be ready to sell your soul for a drop of water or a crumb to eat."

"I won't write it."

"Look here, Hardy. We're not asking very much. All we want you to do is write to your wife that you're safe and tell her to call off the police and those kids of yours. They're too nosy."

"Sooner or later someone is going to trace me here," came Mr. Hardy's faint reply. "And when they do, I can tell them enough to send you to prison for the rest of your life."

There was a sudden commotion in the room and two or three of the smugglers began talking at once.

"You're crazy!" shouted Snattman, but there was a hint of uneasiness in his voice. "You don't know anything about me!"

"I know enough to have you sent up for attempted murder. And you're about to try it again."

"You're too smart, Hardy. That's all the more reason why you're not going to get out of here until we've gone. And if you don't co-operate you'll *never* make it. Our next big shipment's coming through tonight, and then we're skipping the country. If you write that letter, you'll live. If you don't, it's curtains for you!"

Frank and Joe were shaken by the dire threats. But they must decide whether to go for help, or stay and risk capture and try to rescue their father.

"You can't scare me, Snattman," the detective

said. "I have a feeling your time is up. You're never going to get that big shipment."

The detective's voice seemed a little stronger, the boys felt.

Snattman laughed. "I thought you were smart, but you're playing a losing game, I warn you. And how about your family? Are you doing them a service by being so stubborn?"

There was silence for a while. Then Fenton Hardy answered slowly:

"My wife and boys would rather know that I died doing my duty than have me come back to them as a protector of smugglers and criminals."

"You have a very high sense of duty," sneered Snattman. "But you'll change your mind. Are you thirsty?"

There was no reply.

"Are you hungry?"

Still no answer.

"You know you are. And it'll be worse. You'll die of thirst and starvation unless you write that note."

"I'll never write it."

"All right. Come on, men. We'll leave him to himself for a while and give him time to think about it."

Frank squeezed Joe's arm in relief and exhilaration. There was still a chance to save their father!

Footsteps echoed as Snattman and the others

left the room and walked through the corridor. Finally the sounds died away and a door slammed.

Joe made a move toward the door, but Frank held him back. "We'd better wait a minute," he cautioned. "They may have left someone on guard."

The boys stood still, listening intently. But there were no further sounds from beyond the door. At length, satisfied that his father had indeed been left alone, Frank felt for the knob.

Noiselessly he opened the door about an inch, then peered into the corridor which was dimly lighted from one overhead bulb. There was no sign of a guard.

Three doors opened from the corridor—two on the opposite side from where the brothers were standing and another at the end.

The passage was floored with planks and had a beamed ceiling like a cellar. Frank and Joe quickly figured where their father was and sped across the planks to the room. They pushed open the door of the almost dark room and peered inside. There was a crude table and several chairs. In one corner stood a small cot. On it lay Fenton Hardy. He was bound hand and foot to the bed and so tightly trussed that he was unable to move more than a few inches in any direction. He was flat on his back, staring up at the ceiling of his prison. On a chair beside the cot was a sheet of paper and a

pencil, evidently the materials for the letter Snattman had demanded he write.

"Dad!" Frank and Joe cried softly.

The detective had not heard the door open,
but now he looked at his sons in amazement and
relief. "You're here!" he whispered. "Thank
goodness!"

The boys were shocked at the change in their
father's appearance. Normally a rugged-looking
man, Fenton Hardy now was thin and pale. His
cheeks were sunken and his eyes listless.

"We'll have you out of here in a minute," Frank
whispered.

"Hurry!" the detective begged. "Those demons
may be back any minute!"

Frank pulled out his pocketknife and began to
work at the ropes that bound his father. But the
knife was not very sharp and the bonds were thick.

Joe discovered that he did not have his knife
with him. "It probably slipped out of my pocket
when we undressed on the *Napoli*," he said.

"Mine's gone too," Mr. Hardy told them.
"Snattman took everything I had in my pockets,
including concentrated emergency rations. Have
you anything sweet with you?"

Joe pulled out the candy bar from his pocket
and held it, so Mr. Hardy could take a large bite
of the quick-energy food. Meanwhile, his eyes
roamed over the room in search of something

sharp which he might use to help Frank with the ropes. He saw nothing.

Mr. Hardy finished the candy bar, bite by bite. Now Joe started to help Frank by trying to untie the knots. But they were tight and he found it almost impossible to loosen them.

Minutes passed. Frank hacked at the ropes, but the dull blade made little progress. Joe worked at the obstinate knots. Fenton Hardy could give no assistance. All were silent. The only sound was the heavy breathing of the boys and the scraping of the knife against the ropes.

At last Frank was able to saw through one of the bonds and the detective's feet were free. His son pulled the ropes away and began to work on the ones that bound his father's arms. As he reached over with the knife there came a sound that sent a feeling of terror through the Hardys.

It was a heavy footstep beyond the corridor door. Someone was coming back!

Frank worked desperately with the knife, but the ropes still held stubbornly. The dull blade seemed to make almost no impression. But at last a few strands parted. Finally, with Fenton Hardy making a mighty effort and Joe clawing at the rope with his fingers, it snapped.

The detective was free!

But the footfalls of the approaching smuggler came closer.

"Quick!" Frank whispered, as he flung the ropes aside.

"I—I can't hurry!" Mr. Hardy gasped. "I've been tied up so long my feet and legs are numb."

"But we've got to hurry, Dad!" Frank said excitedly. "See if you can stand up."

"I'll—I'll do my best," his father replied, as the boys rubbed his legs vigorously to restore full circulation.

"We must run before those crooks come!" Joe said tensely.

Fenton Hardy got to his feet as hastily as he could. But when he stood up, the detective staggered and would have fallen if Frank had not taken his arm. He was so weak from hunger that a wave of dizziness had come over him. He gave his head a quick shake and the feeling passed.

"All right. Let's go," he said, clinging to both boys for support.

The three hastened out the door of the room and across the corridor to the cave. As they entered it, Mr. Hardy's knees buckled. In desperation his sons picked him up.

"You go on," he whispered. "Leave me here."

"I'm sure all of us can make it," Joe said bravely.

They reached the far door, but the delay had been costly. Just as Frank opened it, clicking off his flashlight, the corridor door was flung open and the ceiling light snapped on.

Frank leaped directly at the smuggler

Frank and Joe had a confused glimpse of the dark man whom they had seen at the pond that afternoon. Snattman! Two rough-looking companions crowded in behind him.

"What's going on here?" Snattman exclaimed, apparently not recognizing the group for a moment.

"It's the Hardys!" one of the other men cried out.

The fleeing trio started down the steps but got no farther than the landing when the smugglers appeared at the stairway and rushed down after them.

"Stop!" cried Snattman, jumping down the last three steps and whipping an automatic from his hip pocket. The place was flooded with light.

As Snattman drew closer, Frank crouched for a spring, then leaped directly at the smuggler. He struck at the man's wrist and the revolver flew out of his grasp. It skidded across the landing and clattered down the steps. Frank closed in on the man. Snattman had been taken completely by surprise. Before he could defend himself, Frank forced him against the wall.

Joe, in the meantime, with a swift uppercut had kayoed one of the other men. And Mr. Hardy, whose strength had partially returned, was battling the third as best he could.

But at this moment the boys saw their father's

adversary dodge to the wall and press a button. In an instant an alarm bell sounded in the corridor. Within seconds a new group of Snattman's gang appeared. As some held drawn revolvers, others overpowered the three Hardys.

In the face of the guns, father and sons were forced to surrender and return to the room where Mr. Hardy had been held captive before.

Within five minutes Fenton Hardy was bound again to the cot, while Frank and Joe, trussed up and unable to move, were tied to two chairs.

CHAPTER XV

Dire Threats

SNATTMAN, once he had recovered from his first consternation and surprise at finding the Hardy boys in the underground room, was in high good humor. He turned to his men.

"Just in time," he gloated, rubbing his hands together in satisfaction. "If we hadn't come here when we did, they'd have all escaped!"

The Hardy boys were silent, sick with despair. They had been sure they were going to succeed in rescuing their father and now the three of them were prisoners of the smuggling gang.

"What are we goin' to do with these guys?" asked one of the men.

The voice sounded familiar to the boys and they looked up. They were not surprised to see that the man was the red-haired one they had met at the

Pollitt place when Frank had discovered his father's cap.

"Do with them?" Snattman mused. "That's a problem. We've got three on our hands now instead of one. Best thing is to leave them all here and lock the door."

"And put gags in their traps," suggested a burly companion.

Red objected. "As long as the Hardys are around here, they're dangerous. They almost got away this time."

"Well, what do you suggest?"

"We ought to do what I wanted to do with the old man in the first place," Red declared doggedly.

"You mean get rid of them?" Snattman asked thoughtfully.

"Sure. All of them!"

"Well—" Snattman gazed at Mr. Hardy with a sinister look.

"I should think you have enough on your conscience already, Snattman!" the detective exclaimed. "I don't expect you to let me go," he added bitterly. "But release my boys. They haven't done anything but try to rescue their father. You'd do the same thing yourself."

"Oh yeah?" Snattman sneered. "Don't bother yourself about my conscience. Nobody—but nobody ever stands in my way.

"As to letting these boys go, what kind of a fool do you take me for?" Snattman shouted. "If you three are such buddies, you ought to enjoy starving together."

The smuggler laughed uproariously at what he considered a very funny remark.

Frank's and Joe's minds were racing with ideas. One thing stood out clearly. Snattman had said the Hardys almost escaped. This meant that no one was guarding the secret entrance!

"If we can only hold out a while," they thought, "the Coast Guard will arrive. There'll be nobody to stop them from coming up here."

Then, suddenly, a shocking possibility occurred to the boys. Suppose the Coast Guard could not find the camouflaged door opening from the pond!

During the conversation four of the smugglers had been whispering among themselves in the corridor. One of them now stepped into the room and faced Snattman.

"I'd like a word with you, chief," he began.

"What is it now?" The smuggler's voice was surly.

"It's about what's to be done with the Hardys, now that we've got 'em," the man said hesitantly. "It's your business what you do to people who make it tough for you when you're on your own. But not in our gang. We're in this for our take out of the smugglin', and we won't stand for too much rough stuff."

"That's right!" one of the other men spoke up.

"Is that so?" Snattman's upper lip curled. "You guys are gettin' awful righteous all of a sudden, aren't you? Look out or I'll dump the lot of you!"

"Oh, no, you won't," replied the first man who had addressed him. "We're partners in this deal and we're goin' to have our full share of what comes in. We ain't riskin' our lives for love, you know."

"We've got another idea about what to do with these three prisoners," a third smuggler spoke up. "I think it's a good one."

"What is it?" Snattman asked impatiently.

"We've been talkin' about Ali Singh."

Frank and Joe started and listened intently.

"What about him?" Snattman prodded his assistant.

"Turn the prisoners over to him. He's got a friend named Foster who's captain of a boat sailin' to the Far East tonight. Put the Hardys on board that ship," the first smuggler urged.

Snattman looked thoughtful. The idea seemed to catch his fancy.

"Not bad," he muttered. "I hadn't thought of Ali Singh. Yes, he'd take care of them. They'd never get back here." He smiled grimly.

"From what he told me about that friend of his,

the captain'd probably dump the Hardys over-board before they got very far out," the man went on smugly. "Seems like he don't feed passengers if he can get rid of 'em!"

"All the better. We wouldn't be responsible."

"Leave them to Ali Singh." Red chuckled evilly. "He'll attend to them."

Snattman walked over to the cot and looked down at Mr. Hardy. "It's too bad your boys had to come barging in here," he said. "Now the three of you will have to take a little ocean voyage." He laughed. "You'll never get to the Coast Guard to tell your story."

The detective was silent. He knew further attempts at persuasion would be useless.

"Well," said Snattman, "haven't you anything to say?"

"Nothing. Do as you wish with me. But let the boys go."

"We'll stick with you, Dad," said Frank quickly.

"Of course!" Joe added.

"You sure will," Snattman declared. "I'm not going to let one of you have the chance of getting back to Bayport with your story."

The ringleader of the smugglers stood in the center of the room for a while, contemplating his captives with a bitter smile. Then he turned suddenly on his heel.

"Well, they're safe enough," he told Red. "We

have that business with Burke to take care of.
Come on, men, load Burke's truck. If any police-
men come along and find it in the lane we'll be
done for."

"How about them?" asked Red, motioning to
the Hardys. "Shouldn't they be guarded?"

"They're tied up tight." Snattman gave a short
laugh. "But I guess we'd better leave one guard,
anyway. Malloy, you stay here and keep watch."

Malloy, a surly, truculent fellow in overalls and
a ragged sweater, nodded and sat down on a box
near the door. This arrangement seemed to
satisfy Snattman. After warning Malloy not to fall
asleep on the job and to see to it that the prisoners
did not escape, he left the room. He was followed
by Red and the other smugglers.

A heavy silence fell over the room after the de-
parture of the men. Malloy crouched gloomily on
the box, gazing blankly at the floor. The butt of a
revolver projected from his hip pocket.

Frank strained against the ropes that bound him
to the chair. But the smugglers had done their
task well. He could scarcely budge.

"We'll never get out of this," he told himself
ruefully.

Joe was usually optimistic but this time his
spirits failed him. "We're in a tough spot," he
thought. "It looks as if we'll all be on that ship
by morning."

To lighten their spirits the Hardys began to talk, hoping against hope to distract the guard and perhaps overpower him.

"Shut up, you guys!" Malloy growled. "Quit your talking or I'll make it hot for you!" He tapped his revolver suggestively.

After that, a melancholy silence fell among the prisoners. All were downhearted. It looked as if their fate truly were sealed.

CHAPTER XVI

Quick Work

IN DESPAIR the boys glanced over at their father on the cot. To their surprise they saw that he was smiling.

Frank was about to ask him what he had found amusing about their predicament when his father shook his head in warning. He looked over at the guard.

Malloy was not watching the prisoners. He sat staring at the floor. Occasionally his head would fall forward, then he would jerk it back as he struggled to keep awake.

"Snattman sure made a poor selection when he chose Malloy as guard," the boys thought.

Several times the burly man straightened up, stretched his arms, and rubbed his eyes. But when he settled down again, his head began to nod.

In the meantime, the boys noticed their father struggling with his bonds. To their amazement he did not seem to be so tightly bound as they had thought. Both of them tried moving but could not budge an inch.

The boys exchanged glances, both realizing what had happened. "Dad resorted to an old trick!" Frank told himself, and Joe was silently fuming, "Why didn't we think of it?"

Mr. Hardy had profited by his previous experience. When the smugglers had seized the detective and tied him to the cot for the second time, he had used a device frequently employed by magicians and professional "escape artists" who boast that they can release themselves from tightly tied ropes and strait jackets.

The detective had expanded his chest and flexed his muscles. He had also kept his arms as far away from his sides as he could without being noticed. In this way, when he relaxed, the ropes did not bind him as securely as his captors intended.

"Oh, why were Frank and I so dumb!" Joe again chided himself.

Frank bit his lip in utter disgust at not having remembered the trick. "But then"—he eased his conscience—"Dad didn't think of it the first time, either."

Mr. Hardy had discovered that the rope binding his right wrist to the cot had a slight slack in it. He began trying to work the rope loose. This took a long time and the rough strands rubbed his wrist raw. But at last he managed to slide his right hand free.

"Hurray!" Frank almost shouted. He glanced at the guard. Malloy appeared to be sound asleep. "Hope he'll stay that way until we can escape," Frank wished fervently.

He and Joe watched their father in amazement, as they saw him grope for one of the knots. The detective fumbled at it for a while. It was slow work with only his one hand free. But the boys knew from his satisfied expression that the smugglers in their haste apparently had not tied the knots as firmly as they should have.

At this instant the guard suddenly lifted his head, and Mr. Hardy quickly laid his free hand back on the cot. He closed his eyes as if sleeping and his sons followed his example. But opening their lids a slit, they watched the smuggler carefully.

The guard grunted. "They're okay," he mumbled. Once more he tried to stay awake but found it impossible. Little by little his head sagged until his chin rested on his chest. Deep, regular breathing told the prisoners he was asleep.

Mr. Hardy now began work again on the knot of the rope that kept his left arm bound to the cot. In a matter of moments he succeeded in loosening it and the rope fell away from his arm.

After making sure the guard was still asleep, the detective sat up on the cot and struggled to release his feet. This was an easier task. The smugglers had merely passed a rope around the cot to hold the prisoner's feet. A few minutes' attention was all that was necessary for the boys' father to work his way loose.

"Now he'll release us," Joe thought excitedly, "and we can escape from here!"

As Fenton Hardy tiptoed toward his sons, the board floor squeaked loudly. The guard muttered again, as if dreaming, shook his head, then sat up.

"Oh, no!" Frank murmured, fearful of what would happen. He saw his father pick up a white rag someone had dropped.

A look of intense amazement crossed Malloy's face. As he opened his mouth to yell for help, Fenton Hardy leaped across the intervening space and flung himself on the smuggler.

"Keep quiet!" the detective ordered.

Malloy had time only to utter a muffled gasp before the detective clapped a hand over the guard's mouth, jammed the rag in it, and toppled him to the floor. The two rolled over and over in a desperate, silent struggle. The boys, helpless, looked on, their fears mounting. They knew their father had been weakened by his imprisonment and hunger, and the guard was strong and muscular. Nevertheless, the detective had the advan-

tage of a surprise attack. Malloy had had no time
to collect his wits.

Frank and Joe watched the battle in an agony
of suspense. If only they could join the fight!

Mr. Hardy still had the advantage, for he could
breathe better than his opponent. But suddenly
Malloy managed to raise himself to his knees. He
reached for the revolver at his hip.

"Look out, Dad!" Frank hissed. "He's got his
gun!"

Quick as a flash the detective landed a blow on
the guard's jaw. Malloy blinked and raised both
hands to defend himself as he fell to the ground.
Mr. Hardy darted forward and pulled the revolver
out of the man's side pocket.

"No funny business!" the detective told him in
a low voice.

Without being told, Malloy raised his hands in
the air. He sat helplessly on the floor, beaten.

"He's got a knife too, Dad," Joe said quietly.
"Watch that."

"Thanks, Joe," his father replied. Then, motioning with the pistol, he said, "All right. Let's
have the knife!"

Sullenly the guard removed the knife from its
leather sheath at his belt and handed it to Mr.
Hardy.

Frank and Joe wanted to shout with joy, but
merely grinned at their father.

Still watching Malloy, the detective walked slowly backward until he reached Joe's side. Without taking his eyes from the smuggler, he bent down and with the knife sliced at the ropes that bound his son. Fortunately, the knife was sharp and the ropes soon were cut.

"Boy, that feels good, Dad. Thanks," Joe whispered.

He sprang from the chair, took the knife, and while his father watched Malloy, he cut Frank's bonds.

"Malloy," Mr. Hardy ordered, "come over here!"

He motioned toward the bed and indicated by gestures that the smuggler was to lie down on the cot. Malloy shook his head vigorously, but was prodded over by Joe. The guard lay down on the cot.

The ropes which had held Mr. Hardy had not been cut. Quickly Frank and Joe trussed up Malloy just as their father had been tied, making certain that the knots were tight. As a final precaution they pushed in the gag which was slipping and with a piece of rope made it secure.

The whole procedure had taken scarcely five minutes. The Hardys were free!

"What now?" Frank asked his father out of earshot of Malloy. "Hide some place until the Coast Guard gets here?" Quickly he told about Tony and Chet going to bring the officers to the smugglers' hide-out.

"But they should have been here by now," Joe whispered. "They probably haven't found the secret door. Let's go down and show them."

This plan was agreed upon, but the three Hardys got no farther than the top of the first stairway when they heard rough, arguing voices below them.

"They can't be Coast Guard men," said Mr. Hardy. "We'll listen a few seconds, then we'd better run in the other direction. I know the way out to the grounds."

From below came an ugly, "You double-crosser, you! This loot belongs to the whole gang and don't you forget it!"

"Listen," said the second voice. "I don't have to take orders from you. I thought we was pals. Now you don't want to go through with the deal. Who's to know if we got ten packages or five from that friend o' Ali Singh's?"

"Okay. And the stuff'll be easier to get rid of than those drugs. They're too hot for me. Snattman can burn for kidnapin' if he wants to—I don't."

The voices had now become so loud that the Hardys did not dare wait another moment. "Come on!" the boys' father urged.

He led the way back to the corridor and along it to the door at the end. Suddenly Frank and Joe noticed him falter and were afraid he was going to faint. Joe recalled that his father had had no food except the candy bar. Ramming his hands into his pockets, he brought out another bar and some pieces of pretzel. Quickly he filled both his father's hands with them. Mr. Hardy ate them hungrily as his sons supported him under his arms and assisted him to the door.

As Frank quietly opened it, and they saw a stairway beyond, the detective said, "These steps will bring us up into a shed near the Pollitt house. There's a trap door. That's the way Snattman brought me down. Got your lights? We haven't any time to lose." Mr. Hardy seemed stronger already. "I'll take the lead."

As they ascended, Frank and Joe wondered if they would come out in the shed where they had seen the man named Klein picking up small logs.

When the detective reached the top of the stairs he ordered the lights out and pushed against the trap door. He could not budge it.

"You try," he urged the boys. "And hurry! Those men we heard may discover Malloy."

"And then things will start popping!" Frank murmured.

The boys heaved their shoulders against the trap door. In a moment there came the rumble of rolling logs. The door went up easily.

Frank peered out. No one seemed to be around.

He stepped up into the shed and the others followed.

The three stood in silence. The night was dark. The wind, blowing through the trees, made a moaning sound. Before the Hardys rose the gloomy mass of the house on the cliff. No lights could be seen.

From the direction of the lane came dull, thudding sounds. The boys and their father assumed the smugglers' truck was being loaded with the goods which were to be disposed of by the man named Burke.

Suddenly the Hardys heard voices from the corridor they had just left. Quickly Frank closed the trap door and Joe piled up the logs. Then, silently, the Hardys stole out into the yard.

CHAPTER XVII

Hostages

LITHE as Indians the three Hardys hurried across the lawn and disappeared among the trees. They headed for the road, a good distance away.

"I hope a bus comes along," Frank said to himself. "Then we can get to a phone and report—"

His thought was rudely interrupted as the boys and their father heard a sound that struck terror to their hearts—the clatter of the logs tumbling off the trap door!

An instant later came a hoarse shout. "Chief! Red! The Hardys got away! Watch out for them!"

"He must be one of the men we heard coming up from the shore," Joe decided. "They must have found Malloy trussed up!"

Instantly the place became alive with smugglers flashing their lights. Some of the men ran from the truck toward the road, shouting. Others began to comb the woods. Another man emerged from the trap door. He and his companion dashed to the ocean side of the house.

Two burly smugglers flung open the kitchen door and ran out. One shouted, "They ain't in the house!"

"And they're not down at the shore!" the other yelled. "I just talked to Klein on the phone down there."

"You guys better not let those Hardys get away!" Snattman's voice cut through the night. "It'll be the pen for all of you!"

"Fenton Hardy's got a gun! He took Malloy's!" came a warning voice from the far side of the house. The two men who had gone to the front now returned. "He never misses his mark!"

When the fracas had started, the detective had pulled his sons to the ground, told them to lie flat, face down, and not to move. Now they could hear the pounding steps of the smugglers as they dashed among the trees. The boys' hearts pounded wildly. It did not seem possible they could be missed!

Yet man after man ran within a few yards of the three prone figures and dashed on toward the road. Presently Mr. Hardy raised his head and looked toward the Pollitt mansion.

"Boys," he said tensely, "we'll make a run for

the kitchen door. The men won't expect us to go there."

The three arose. Swiftly and silently they crossed the dark lawn and slipped into the house. Apparently no one had seen them.

"When Snattman doesn't find us outdoors," Joe whispered, "won't he look here to make sure?"

"Yes," Mr. Hardy replied. "But by that time I hope the Coast Guard and State Police will arrive."

"Joe and I found a hidden stairway to the attic," Frank spoke up. "Snattman won't think of looking in it. Let's hide up there."

"You forget the ghost," Joe reminded his brother. "*He* knows we found that stairway."

"Nevertheless, Frank's suggestion is a good one," Mr. Hardy said. "Let's go to the attic. Were any clothes hanging in the closet that might be used to conceal the door?"

"Yes, a man's bathrobe on a rod."

The Hardys did not dare use a light and had to make their way along by feeling walls, and the stair banister, with Frank in the lead and Mr. Hardy between the boys. Reaching the second floor, Frank looked out the rear window of the hall.

"The smugglers are coming back!" he remarked in a low voice. "The lights are heading this way!"

The Hardys doubled their speed, but it was still slow going, for they banged into chairs and a wardrobe as Frank felt his way along the hall toward the bedroom where the hidden staircase was.

Finally the trio reached it. Just as Frank was about to open the door to the attic, a door on the first floor swung open with a resounding bang.

"Scatter and search every room!" Snattman's crisp voice rang out.

"We're trapped!" Joe groaned.

"Maybe not," Frank said hopefully. "I have a hunch Klein was the ghost. It's possible that he's the only one who knows about this stairway and he's down at the shore."

"We'll risk going up," Mr. Hardy decided. "But not a sound." He slid the bathrobe across the rod, so that it would hide the door.

"The stairs creak," Joe informed him.

Mr. Hardy told his sons to push down the treads slowly but firmly with their hands and hold them there until they put one foot between them and then raised up to their full weight.

"And lean forward, so you won't lose your balance," he warned.

Fearful that he could not accomplish this, Frank opened the door carefully and started up in the pitch blackness. But the dread thought of capture made him use extreme caution and he reached the attic without having made a sound.

After closing the door, Joe and his father quickly followed. The three moved noiselessly to a spot out of sight of the stairway behind a large trunk.

They sat down and waited, not daring even to whisper. From downstairs they could hear running footsteps, banging doors, and loud talk.

"Not here!"

"Not here!"

"Not here!"

The search seemed to come to an end, for the second-floor group had gathered right in the room where the secret stairway was.

"This is it! The end! They're going to search up here!" Frank thought woefully.

His father reached over and grasped a hand of each of his sons in a reassuring grip. Someone yanked open the closet door. The Hardys became tense. Would the robe over the entrance to the secret stairway fool him?

"Empty!" the man announced and shut the door. The smugglers went downstairs.

There were fervent handshakes among the detective and his sons. Other than this they did not move a muscle of their bodies, although they inwardly relaxed.

Now new worries assailed the Hardys. It was possible that Snattman and his gang, having been alerted, would move out and disappear before the police or Coast Guard could get to the house on the cliff.

Frank's heart gave a jump. He suddenly realized that his father was hiding to protect his sons. Had he been alone, the intrepid detective would have been downstairs battling to get the better of Snattman and break up the smuggling ring.

"What a swell father he is!" Frank thought. Then another idea came to him. "Maybe being here isn't such a bad plan after all. Dad might have been fatally shot if he'd been anywhere else on the property."

A moment later the Hardys again became aware of voices on the second floor. They recognized one as Snattman's, the other as Klein's.

"Yeah, there's a secret stairway to the attic," Klein announced. "I found it when I was playin' ghost. And them Hardy boys—they found it too. I'll bet my last take on those rare drugs we're gettin' tonight that the dick and his sons are up in that attic!"

The Hardys' spirits sank. They were going to be captured again after all!

They heard the door at the foot of the stairway open. "Go up and look, Klein," ordered Snattman.

"Not me. Fenton Hardy has Malloy's gun."

"I said go up!"

"You can't make me," Klein objected in a whining tone. "I'd be a sure target 'cause I couldn't see him. He'd be hiding and let me have it so quick I'd never know what hit me."

Despite the grave situation, Frank's and Joe's

faces were creased in smiles, but they faded as Snattman said, "I'll go myself. Give me that big light!"

Suddenly a brilliant beam was cast into the attic. It moved upward, accompanied by heavy footsteps.

"Hardy, if you want to live, say so!" Snattman said, an evil ring in his voice.

No answer from the detective.

"We've got you cornered this time!"

Mr. Hardy did not reply.

"Listen, Hardy!" Snattman shouted. "I know you're up there because you moved that bathrobe. I'll give you just one minute to come down out of that attic!"

Still no answer and an interval of silence followed.

Then came Snattman's voice again. "This is your last chance, Hardy!"

Nearly a minute went by without a sign from the two enemy camps. Then Snattman moved up the stairs a few more steps.

"Hardy, I have a proposition to make to you," he said presently. "I know you don't want to die and you want those boys of yours to live too. Well, so do I want to live. So let's call it quits."

The detective maintained his silence and Snattman continued up the steps. "Give you my

"You are my hostages!" the smuggler sneered

word I won't shoot. And I know you never fire first unless you have to."

A moment later he appeared at the top of the stairs, empty-handed except for the light. In a moment he spotted the Hardys with his high-powered flashlight.

"Here's the proposition—your lives in exchange for mine and my gang's."

"How do you mean?" Mr. Hardy asked coldly.

"I mean," the smuggler said, "that you are my hostages."

"Hostages!" Frank and Joe exclaimed together.

"Yes. If my men and I can get our stuff moved away before the police or the Coast Guard might happen in here, then you can leave a little later."

"But if they do come?" Frank asked.

"Then I'll bargain with them," Snattman answered. "And I don't think they'll turn me down. They don't know where you are, but I'll make them understand I mean business. If they take me, you three die!"

Frank and Joe gasped. The famous Fenton Hardy and his sons were to be used as a shield to protect a ruthless gang of criminals!

The boys looked at their father in consternation. To their amazement he looked calm, but his mouth was drawn in a tight line.

"It won't do you any good to shoot me, Hardy," the smuggler said. "Mallory said all the chambers in that gat are empty but one. If the gang hears a shot, they'll be up here in a minute to finish you all off properly."

The Hardys realized that if Snattman's remark about the gun were true, they were indeed at the mercy of this cunning, scheming, conniving smuggler. He now started backing toward the stairway.

"I think I'm a pretty fair guy," he said with the trace of a satisfied smile.

"And one to be hated and feared!" Joe thought in a rage. "We've *got* to outwit this man somehow!" he determined.

But at the moment the possibility of this looked hopeless.

CHAPTER XVIII

Coast Guard Action

WHILE the Hardy boys had been investigating the smugglers' hide-out and had been captured, together with their father, Tony and Chet were trying their best to accomplish the errand which Frank and Joe had given them.

During the early part of their trip back to Bayport to contact the Coast Guard, the *Napoli* had cut through the darkness like a streak. Then suddenly Tony exclaimed, "Oh, oh! My starboard light just went out."

Chet turned to look at the portside. "This light's all right. Must be the bulb in the other one."

"That's what I was afraid of," said Tony. "I'll bet I haven't another bulb."

"You mean, somebody might not see the *Napoli* and ram us?" Chet asked fearfully.

"We'll have to be careful," Tony replied.

"Chet, take the wheel, will you? I'll see if I can find an extra bulb."

Chet changed places with Tony, throttled the motor, and gazed intently ahead. The moon had not yet risen and it was difficult to see very far ahead.

"Find anything?" Chet called out, as Tony finished his round of the lockers and was now rummaging in the last one.

"Not yet." Tony pulled out a canvas bag, a pair of sneakers, and some fishing tackle. As he reached in for the last article in the locker, he gave a whoop of joy. "Here's one bulb—just one—keep your fingers crossed, pal. If this isn't any good, we're in a mess."

"And breaking the law besides," Chet added.

He held his breath as Tony went forward and crawled inside the prow of the *Napoli*. With a flashlight, Tony found the protecting shield for the bulb and unfastened it. After removing the dead bulb, he screwed in the new one. As the light flashed on, Tony breathed a sigh of relief and started to crawl out of the prow.

"Good work!" Chet said. "It's lucky we—"

Chet never finished the sentence. At this instant he saw another speedboat loom up in front of him. Like lightning he swung the wheel around, missing the oncoming craft by inches!

"You fool!" the driver of the other boat

shouted. "Why don't you look where you're going?"

Chet did not reply. He was quivering. Besides, he had stalled the motor, which had been throttled so low it had not been able to take the terrific swerving. "Oh, now I've done it!" the stout boy wailed.

There was no response from Tony for several seconds. He had been thrown violently against the side of the boat and was dazed. But he quickly collected his wits and crawled down beside Chet.

"What happened?" he asked.

Chet told him, then said, "You'd better take over. I'm a rotten pilot."

Tony took the seat behind the wheel, started the motor, and sped off toward Barmet Bay.

"We've sure wasted a lot of time," he remarked. "I wonder how Frank and Joe are making out."

"Hope they found Mr. Hardy," Chet added.

There was no more conversation until the boys turned into the bay. The Coast Guard station for the area was a short distance along the southern shore of the bay and Tony headed the *Napoli* directly for it. He pulled up at the dock, where two patrol boats and a cutter were tied.

The two boys climbed out and hurried up to the white building. As they were about to enter it, Chet and Tony were amazed to find Biff Hooper and Phil Cohen coming out of it. Jerry Gilroy, another Bayport High friend, was with them.

"Well, for Pete's sake!" the three cried out, and Biff added, "Boy, are we glad to see you! Where are Frank and Joe?"

"Still hunting for the smugglers," Chet replied. "What brings you here?"

Biff explained that an hour ago Mrs. Hardy had telephoned him to see if he had heard from Frank and Joe. She confessed to being exceedingly worried about her sons. Mrs. Hardy knew they had gone to look for their father and she was in a panic that they had been captured by the same men who were possibly holding her husband.

"I told her I'd round up a couple of the fellows and go on a hunt," Biff went on. "Jerry thought maybe Frank and Joe had come back to town and were somewhere around. We looked, but we couldn't find them anywhere, so we borrowed Mr. Gilroy's car and came out here to tell the Coast Guard. They're going to send out boats. You'd better come in and talk to Chief Warrant Officer Robinson yourself."

The boys hurried inside. Quickly Chet and Tony told of the Hardys' suspicion that they had found the entrance to the smugglers' hide-out.

"Can you send help out there right away?" Chet asked. "We'll show you where the secret tunnel is."

"This is astounding," said Chief Robinson. "I'll order the *Alice* out. You can start within five minutes."

"I'll phone Mrs. Hardy right away," Jerry offered. "I'm afraid, though, that the news isn't going to make her feel too good."

While Jerry was gone, Chet told the chief warrant officer that the Hardys thought they knew the names of two of the men who were involved in the smuggling racket. Chet revealed the Hardy suspicions about Snattman being one and Ali Singh the other.

"We think Ali is a crewman on the *Marco Polo* that's going to dock early tomorrow morning in Bayport," Chet continued. "Frank and Joe got a tip that makes them think this is the deal: While the ship is offshore, Ali Singh pitches stolen drugs overboard and one of the smugglers picks the package up in a speedboat."

Robinson raised his eyebrows. "Those Hardy boys certainly take after their father," he remarked. "They have the makings of good detectives."

Biff told the Coast Guard officer of the boys' adventure at the haunted house on their first visit to the Pollitt place. "Frank and Joe are sure there is some connection between the house and the smugglers."

"And they are probably right," the chief remarked. "I'll call the State Police at once and tell them the latest developments in this case."

The boys waited while he made the report. Jerry, who had just finished telephoning Mrs. Hardy, said that she seemed even more worried than before but relieved that the Coast Guard was going to take a hand.

The chief warrant officer then told the boys he would get in touch with the captain of the *Marco Polo* at once by ship-to-shore telephone. The connection was made and the boys listened with great interest to the conversation. The captain had a booming voice which they could hear plainly.

"Yes, I have a sailor named Ali Singh," he replied in answer to Chief Robinson's question. "He's a member of the kitchen crew."

After he had been told that Ali Singh was suspected of stealing drug shipments and dropping them overboard to a confederate, he said, "That would be pretty easy for him to do. Singh probably throws them out when he dumps garbage into the water, even though he's not supposed to do it. The drugs could be in an inflated waterproof bag."

"Captain, will you have someone keep an eye on this Ali Singh without his knowing he's being watched?" Chief Robinson requested. "I'll send a patrol boat out from here to watch for any of his gang who may be in a small boat waiting to pick up something he dumps overboard. How far offshore are you?"

"About sixteen miles from your headquarters," was the answer.

"Will you keep in touch with the patrol boat?" Robinson requested. "It's the *Henley*, in charge of Chief Petty Officer Brown."

"I'll do that."

"Ali Singh can be arrested when your ship docks."

As the conversation was concluded, a uniformed coastguardman came in. He was introduced as Chief Petty Officer Bertram in charge of the *Alice*, which would follow Tony and Chet to the smugglers' hide-out.

"I'm ready, sir," he told his chief, after a short briefing. He turned to the boys. "All set?"

Chet and Tony nodded. As they turned to follow Bertram, Biff, Phil, and Jerry looked glum.

Noting the expressions on the three boys, Chief Robinson leaned across his desk and said, "I guess you fellows were hoping to be in on this too. How would you like to go on the *Henley* with Chief Petty Officer Brown and watch the fun?"

The eyes of the three boys lighted up and Phil said, "You mean it?"

"Do you want a formal invitation?" Chief Robinson asked with a laugh.

He rang for Chief Petty Officer Brown, and after introducing the boys, he explained what the mission of the *Henley* was to be.

"I understand, sir," Brown replied. "We'll leave at once."

The three boys followed him down to the dock and went aboard. They met the other Coast Guard men and the fast patrol boat set off. It seemed to the boys as if the sixteen miles were covered in an incredibly short time. The lights of the *Marco Polo* loomed up in the distance.

"She's moving very slowly, isn't she?" Biff asked their skipper.

"Yes, she's making only about four knots."

"So it would be easy for a small boat to come alongside and take something from her?" Phil suggested.

"Yes, it would." Quickly the officer picked up a telescope and trained it on the large craft. "The galley hatches are on the left and the tide is coming in," he reported. "Anything thrown overboard will float toward shore."

He ordered the wheelsman to go past the *Marco Polo,* come down the other side, and approach within three hundred yards, then turn off the engine and lights.

When they reached the designated spot, Petty Officer Brown ordered everyone on board the *Henley* not to talk or to move around. The *Marco*

Polo's decks, as well as the water some distance from the craft, was illuminated by light from some of the stateroom portholes. Biff, Phil, and Jerry crowded close to the chief as he trained his powerful binoculars on the galley hatches, so he could give them a running account of anything that might happen. The officer reported little activity aboard the *Marco Polo* and the boys assumed that the passengers either were asleep or packing their luggage in anticipation of landing the next morning.

Suddenly Petty Officer Brown saw one of the hatches open. A small man, with a swarthy complexion and rather longish coal-black hair, appeared in the circular opening. He looked out, then raised a large pail and dumped its contents into the water. Quickly he closed the hatch.

"Ali Singh!" the three boys thought as Brown reported what he had seen.

They watched excitedly to see what would happen now.

Suddenly Biff grabbed Phil's arm and pointed. Vaguely they could see a long pole with a scooping net fastened to the end of it appear from outside the circle of light and fish among the debris. Petty Officer Brown reported that apparently the person holding the pole had found what he wanted, for he scooped something up and the pole vanished from sight.

The boys strained their ears for the sound of a small boat. It did not come and they were puzzled. They also wondered why Petty Officer Brown seemed to be doing nothing about trying to apprehend the person.

The tense skipper suddenly handed the binoculars to Phil. Without a word the puzzled boy looked through them at the spot where Brown had been gazing. To his amazement he could make out the dim shape of a speedboat with two figures in it. Each held an oar and was rowing the small boat away from the *Marco Polo* as fast as possible.

"We've got the smugglers dead to rights!" Petty Officer Brown whispered to the boys.

"Aren't you going to arrest them?" Phil asked.

"Not yet," the officer told him. "I'm afraid we can't do it without some shooting. I don't want to scare the passengers on the *Marco Polo*. We'll wait a few minutes."

Suddenly the engine of the smugglers' speedboat was started. Tersely, Brown began issuing orders to his men. The motors roared into action.

The chase was on!

CHAPTER XIX

The Chase

In a few minutes the *Henley's* brilliant searchlight was turned on. It picked up the speedboat which was racing toward shore at full power. But gradually the Coast Guard boat lessened the distance between them.

Chief Petty Officer Brown picked up a megaphone and shouted for the fleeing men to stop. They paid no attention.

"We'll have to show them we mean business," the officer told Biff, Phil, and Jerry. "We'll shoot across their bow."

He ordered the boys out of the line of fire, in case the smugglers should attempt to retaliate. They obeyed, and though from their shelter the three could not see the speedboat, they listened intently to what was going on.

The *Henley* plowed ahead and presently the boys heard a shot whistle through the air.

"Stop your engine!" Brown commanded. A second later he added, "Drop those guns!"

The smugglers evidently did both, for Skipper Brown said to the boys, "You fellows can come forward now."

The three scrambled to his side. Biff was just in time to see one of the two captured men half turn and slyly run his hand into the large pocket of his sports jacket. Biff expected him to pull out a gun and was about to warn Brown when the smuggler withdrew his hand and dropped something into the water.

"The rare drugs!" Biff thought.

Instantly he began peeling off his clothes, and when the others asked him what he was doing this for, he merely said, "Got an underwater job to do."

Biff was over the side in a flash and swimming with strong, long strokes to the speedboat. He went beyond it and around to the far side.

In the meantime, Petty Officer Brown had ordered the smugglers to put their hands over their heads. As the *Henley* came alongside, two of the enlisted coastguardmen jumped across and slipped handcuffs on them. Brown instructed one of the enlisted men to take their prisoners back to Coast Guard headquarters in the smugglers' boat.

"You got nothin' on us! You ain't got no right to arrest us!" one of the captured men cried out.

At that moment Biff Hooper's head appeared over the side of the speedboat and a moment later he clambered aboard. He called out, "You've got plenty on these men! Here's the evidence!"

He held up a waterproof bag, tightly sealed. It was transparent and the printing on the contents was easily read. "I happen to know that what's in here is a rare drug," Biff added. "I heard our doctor mention it just a few days ago."

This announcement took the bravado out of the smugglers. The two men insisted they were only engaged to pilot the speedboat and deliver the drugs. But they would not give the name of the person who had hired them, nor the spot to which they were supposed to go.

"We know both the answers already," Petty Officer Brown told the smugglers. Then he said to his wheelsman, "Head for the house on the cliff! They may need a little more help over there."

Biff was hauled aboard, and as he put his clothes back on, the *Henley* shot through the water. He whispered to his pals, "We'll see some more excitement, maybe."

Some time before this, Chet and Tony had reached the area where the secret tunnel was. The patrol boat which had been following them turned on its great searchlight to pick out the exact spot.

"Look!" Chet cried out.

A speedboat with two men in it had just entered

the choppy, rocky waters in front of the tunnel.

"Halt!" Skipper Bertram of the *Alice* ordered.

The man at the wheel obeyed the command and turned off his motor. But instead of surrendering, he shouted to his companion, "Dive, Sneffen!"

Quick as a flash the two smugglers disappeared into the water on the far side of their boat. When they did not reappear, Chet called:

"I'll bet they're swimming underwater to the tunnel. Aren't we going after them?"

"We sure are," Petty Officer Bertram replied. "Tony, can you find the channel which leads to that tunnel?"

"I think so," Tony answered, eying the smugglers' speedboat which now, unattended, had been thrown violently by the waves onto some rocks.

"Then we'll come on board your boat," the chief petty officer stated. He left two of his own men aboard the *Alice* to guard it and to be ready for any other smugglers who might be arriving at the hide-out.

The rest of the crew, including Bertram himself, climbed aboard the *Napoli*, and Tony started through the narrow passage between the rocks leading to the tunnel. One of the enlisted men in the prow of the boat operated a portable searchlight. Everyone kept looking for the swimmers, as they went through the tunnel, but did not see them. When the *Napoli* reached the pond, the man swung his light around the circular shore line.

"There they are!" Chet cried out.

The two smugglers, dripping wet, had just opened the secret door into the cliff. They darted through and the door closed behind them.

Tony pulled his boat to the ledge in front of the door, turned off the engine, and jumped ashore with the others. To their surprise the door was not locked.

"I'll go first," Bertram announced.

"But be careful!" Chet begged. "There may be a man with a gun on the other side!"

The officer ordered everyone to stand back as he pulled the door open. He beamed the searchlight inside. No one was in sight!

"Come on, men!" the skipper said excitedly.

The group quickly went along the route the Hardys had discovered earlier. When they reached the corridor and saw the three doors, Tony suggested that they look inside to see if the Hardys were prisoners. One by one each room was examined but found to be empty.

The searchers hurried on down the corridor and up the stairway which led to the woodshed of the Pollitt place. They pushed the trap door but it did not open. Their light revealed no hidden springs or catches.

"The two smugglers that got away from us may have sounded an alarm," Bertram said. "They probably set something heavy on top of this trap door to delay us."

"Then we'll heave it off!" Chet declared.

He and Tony, with two of the enlisted men, put their shoulders to the trap door and heaved with all their might. At last it raised a little, then fell back into place.

"It isn't nailed shut from the other side at any rate," Bertram said. "Give it another shove!"

The four beneath it tried once more. Now they all could hear something sliding sideways.

"All together now!" Chet said, puffing. "One, two, three!"

The heave that followed did the trick. A heavy object above toppled with a crash, and the trap door opened. As before, Chief Petty Officer Bertram insisted upon being the first one out. There was not a sound from the grounds nor the house and not a light in evidence. He told the others to come up but cautioned:

"This may be an ambush. Watch your step and if anything starts to pop, you two boys go back down through the trap door."

Suddenly there was a sound of cars turning into the lane leading to the Pollitt place. The vehicles' lights were so bright that Bertram said, "I believe it's the police!"

A few moments later the cars reached the rear of the old house and state troopers piled out. Chief

Petty Officer Bertram hurried forward to introduce himself to Captain Ryder of the State Police. The two held a whispered conversation. From what the boys overheard, they figured that the troopers planned to raid the house.

Just as the men seemed to have reached a decision, everyone was amazed to see a man appear at the rear window of the second-floor hall. He held a gun in his right hand, but with his left he gestured for attention.

"My name's Snattman," he announced with a theatrical wave of his hand. "Before you storm this place, I want to talk to you! I know you've been looking for me and my men a long time. But I'm not going to let you take me without some people on your side getting killed first!" He paused dramatically.

"Come to the point, Snattman," Captain Ryder called up to him. He, too, had a gun poised for action should this become necessary.

"I mean," the smuggler cried out, "that I got three hostages in this house—Fenton Hardy and his two sons!"

Chet and Tony jumped. The boys had found their father, only to become captives themselves. And now the three were to be used as hostages!

"What's the rest?" Captain Ryder asked acidly.

"This: If you'll let me and my men go, we'll clear out of here. One will stay behind long

enough to tell you where the Hardys are." Snattman now set his jaw. "But if you come in and try
to take us, it'll be curtains for the Hardys!"

Chet's and Tony's hearts sank. What was going
to be the result of this nightmarish dilemma?

In the meantime Frank, Joe, and their father,
for the past hour, had despaired of escaping before
Snattman might carry out his sinister threat. After
the smuggler left the attic, they had heard ham-
mering and suspected the smugglers were nailing
bars across the door. The Hardys tiptoed to the
foot of the stairway, only to find their fears con-
firmed.

"If those bars are made of wood," Frank whispered, "maybe we can cut through them with our
knives without too much noise."

"We'll try," his father agreed. "Joe, take that
knife I got from Malloy."

As Detective Hardy sat on the steps, leaning
weakly against the wall, his two sons got to work.
They managed to maneuver the knives through
the crack near the knob. Finding the top of the
heavy crossbars, the boys began to cut and hack
noiselessly. Frank's knife was already dull and it
was not long before Joe's became so. This greatly
hampered their progress.

Half an hour later the boys' arms were aching
so badly that Frank and Joe wondered how they
could continue. But the thought that their lives

were at stake drove them on. They would rest for two or three minutes, then continue their efforts. Finally Joe finished cutting through one bar and started on the second of the three they had found. Ten minutes later Frank managed to cut through his.

"Now we can take turns," he told his brother.

Working this way, with rest periods in between, the boys found the task less arduous.

"We're almost free!" Joe finally said hopefully.

Just then, the Hardys heard cars coming into the driveway. They were sure that the police had arrived because of the illumination flooding the place even to the crack under the attic door.

It was less than a minute later that they heard the cars come to a stop outside and then Snattman's voice bargaining for his own life in exchange for his hostages!

"Let's break this door down and take our chances," Frank whispered hoarsely.

"No!" his father said. "Snattman and his men would certainly shoot us!"

At this instant Frank gave a low cry of glee. His knife had just hacked through the last wooden bar. Turning the knob, he opened the door and the three Hardys stole silently from their prison.

From the bedroom doorway they peered out to where Snattman was still trying to bargain with the police. No one else was around. The boys and their father looked at one another, telegraphing a common thought.

They would rush the king of the smugglers and overpower him!

CHAPTER XX

The Smuggler's Request

As THE three Hardys crept forward, hoping to over-power Snattman before he saw them, they heard a voice outside the house say, "You'll never get away with this, Snattman! You may as well give up without any shooting!"

"I'll never give up!"

"The house is surrounded with troopers and Coast Guard men!"

"What do I care?" Snattman shouted, waving his arms out the window. "I got three hostages here, and I've got one of the Coast Guard."

"He's in the house too?"

Snattman laughed. "Trying to catch me, eh? Well, I'm not going to answer that question."

There was silence outside the house. This seemed to worry the man. He cried out, "It won't do you any good to talk things over! I got you where I want you and—"

Like three stalking panthers Frank, Joe, and their father pounced upon the unwary smuggler. Mr. Hardy knocked the man's gun from his hand. It flew out the window and thudded to the ground below. The boys pinned his arms back and buckled in his knees.

From below came a whoop of joy. "The Hardys have captured Snattman!" The voice was Chet Morton's.

"My men will never let you in here!" the victim screamed. He snarled, twisted, and turned in his captors' grip.

Mr. Hardy, fearful that Snattman would shout to order his men upstairs, clamped a hand over the smuggler's mouth. By this time there was terrific confusion inside and outside the Pollitt place. State troopers and the Coast Guard men had burst into both the front and rear doors.

Others guarded the sides of the house to prevent any escape from the windows. A few shots were fired, but soon the smuggling gang gave up without fighting further. The capture of their leader and the sudden attack had unnerved them.

The Hardys waited upstairs with their prisoner. In a few moments Chet and Tony appeared and behind them, to the utter astonishment of Frank and Joe, were Biff, Phil, and Jerry.

Stories were quickly exchanged and Mr. Hardy praised Frank's and Joe's chums for their efforts.

All this time Snattman glowered maliciously.

In a few moments chief petty officers Bertram and Brown appeared in the second-floor hall with Captain Ryder. Immediately the state trooper fastened handcuffs onto the prisoner. He was about to take him away when Frank spoke up:

"There's someone else involved in this smuggling who hasn't been captured yet."

"You mean the man who got away from here in the truck?" Officer Ryder asked. "We've set up a roadblock for him and expect to capture him any minute."

Frank shook his head. "Ali Singh, the crewman on the *Marco Polo,* has a friend who owns a small cargo ship. Right now, it's lying somewhere offshore. Snattman was thinking of putting my dad, Joe, and me on it and arranging things so that we never got home again."

The king of the smugglers, who had been silent for several minutes, now cried out, "You're crazy! There's not a word of truth in it! There isn't any boat offshore!"

The others ignored the man. As soon as he stopped yelling, Joe took up the story. "I have a hunch you'll find that your Coast Guard man is a prisoner on that cargo ship. The name of the captain is Foster."

"You mean our man Ayres is on that ship?" Petty Officer Brown asked unbelievingly.

"We don't know anyone named Ayres," Frank began. He stopped short and looked at his brother. They nodded significantly at each other, then Frank asked, "Does Ayres go under the name of Jones?"

"He might, if he were cornered. You see, he's sort of a counterspy for the Coast Guard. He pretended to join the smugglers and we haven't heard from him since Saturday."

"I found out about him," Snattman bragged. "That name Jones didn't fool us. I saw him make a sneak trip to your patrol boat."

Frank and Joe decided this was the scene they had seen through the telescope. They told about their rescue of "Jones" after a hand grenade had nearly killed him. They also gave an account of how his kidnapers had come to the Kane farmhouse, bound up the farmer and his wife, and taken "Jones."

Skipper Brown said he would send a patrol boat out to investigate the waters in the area and try to find Captain Foster's ship.

"We'll wait here for you," Captain Ryder stated. "This case seems to be one for both our branches of service. Two kidnapings on land and a theft from the *Marco Polo,* as well as an undeclared vessel offshore."

While he was gone, the Hardys attempted to question Snattman. He refused to admit any guilt in connection with smuggling operations or the shipment of stolen goods from one state to another. Frank decided to talk to him along different lines, hoping that the smuggler would inadvertently confess something he did not intend to.

"I heard you inherited this house from your uncle, Mr. Pollitt," Frank began.

"That's right. What's it to you?"

Frank was unruffled. "I was curious about the tunnel and the stairways and the cave," he said pleasantly. "Did your uncle build them?"

Snattman dropped his sullen attitude. "No, he didn't," the smuggler answered. "My uncle found them all by accident. He started digging through his cellar wall to enlarge the place, and broke right through to that corridor."

"I see," said Frank. "Have you any idea who did build it?"

Snattman said that his uncle had come to the conclusion that the tunnel and pond had been discovered by pirates long, long ago. They apparently had decided it would be an ideal hide-out and had built the steps all the way to the top of the ground.

"Of course the woodshed wasn't there then," Snattman explained. "At least not the one that's here now. The trap door was, though, but there was a tumble-down building over it."

"How about the corridor? Was it the same size when your uncle found it?"

"Yes," the smuggler answered. "My uncle figured that was living quarters for the pirates when they weren't on their ship."

"Pretty fascinating story," Tony Prito spoke up.

Several seconds of silence followed. Snattman's eyes darted from one boy to another. Finally they fastened on Frank Hardy and he said:

"Now that I'm going to prison, the eyepieces to your telescope, and your motorcycle tools, won't do me any good. You'll find them in a drawer in the kitchen."

"Thanks a lot," said Frank.

There was another short silence. Then the smuggler went on, his head down and his eyes almost closed, "Mr. Hardy, I envy you. And I—I never thought I'd be making this kind of a confession. You know almost everything about what I've been doing. I'll tell the whole story later. Since they're going to find that Coast Guard officer, Ayres, on Foster's ship there's no use in my holding out any longer.

"I said I envy you, Mr. Hardy. It's because you brought up two such fine boys and they got swell friends. Me—I wasn't so lucky. My father died when I was little. I was pretty headstrong and my mother couldn't manage me. I began to make the wrong kind of friends and after that—you know how it is.

"My uncle, who owned this place, might have helped me, but he was mean and selfish and never gave us any money. The most he would do was invite my mother and me here once in a while for a short visit. I hated him because he made my mother work very hard around the house all the time we were here. It wasn't any vacation for her.

"One of the times when I was here my uncle showed me the pirates' hide-out and I never forgot it. After I got in with a gang of hoods I kept thinking about this place, and what a swell hide-out it would be for smugglers. I was afraid to try it while my uncle was alive. But when I heard he was dead, I thought that was my chance.

"You see, I didn't dare go to claim the property as the rightful heir. But now I'm planning to take it over. Of course it won't do me any good, because I know I'll have to do a long stretch in the pen. But I'm going to ask those executors to use my uncle's money to run this place as a boys' home—I mean a place where boys without proper home training can come to live."

The group listening to Snattman, king of the smugglers, were too overwhelmed by his complete change of heart to say anything for a few seconds. But when the man looked up, as if pleading for his hearers to believe him, Mr. Hardy said, "That's a very fine thing for you to do, Snattman. I'm sure that the boys who benefit from living here will always be grateful to you."

The solemn scene was suddenly interrupted by the return of Chief Petty Officer Brown. He reported that another patrol boat had picked up his message about Captain Foster's ship and within a few minutes had reported sighting it. Then, within a quarter of an hour, word came that Captain Foster had been put under arrest, and that the missing Coast Guard man had been found on the ship, as well as a quantity of merchandise which the captain had expected Snattman to remove.

The prisoners were now taken away from the Pollitt home and the Hardys and their friends found themselves alone.

Chet asked suddenly, "How do we get home?"

Tony grinned. "I guess the *Napoli* will hold all of us."

The group went to the woodshed, opened the trap door, and started down the secret passageway to the pond below. They climbed into the *Napoli* and Tony slipped behind the wheel. The Coast Guard men thoughtfully had left the portable searchlight on the prow and Tony was able to make the trip through the tunnel and the narrow channel out to the ocean without accident.

Suddenly Frank spoke up, "Dad, what happened to your car?"

Mr. Hardy smiled. "It's in Bayport in a garage. I was being followed, so I shook off the shadowers and took the bus." He added ruefully, "But it didn't do me much good. Snattman's men attacked me and took me prisoner on the road."

The famous detective now said, "While I have the chance, I want to thank each of you boys individually for what you did. Without the seven of you, this case might never have been solved and I might not have been found alive."

Modestly Frank and Joe and their friends acknowledged the praise, secretly hoping another mystery would come their way soon. One did and by learning *The Secret of the Old Mill* the Hardy boys encountered a cunning gang of counterfeiters.

Suddenly Joe remarked, "Compliments are flying around here pretty thick, but there's one person we forgot to mention. Without him, Frank and I might never have found Dad."

"Who's that?" Biff asked.

"Pretzel Pete!" Joe replied.

"That's right," said Frank. "All together, fellows! A rousing cheer for Pretzel Pete!"